JF
Pease Ghost Over
Gow der Creek

DATE DUE			
APR 06			
JAN 2 7 2016			

Ghost Over Boulder Creek

A Historical Cheyenne Mystery

Ghost Over Boulder Creek

A Historical Cheyenne Mystery

By
Elaine Pease

ISBN: 978-0-86541-104-3 (hardcover edition)
Library of Congress Control Number: 2010931513

Copyright © 2010 Elaine Pease ALL RIGHTS RESERVED
Cover illustration © 2010 Cathy Morrison
Book design by Kooima Kreations, Colorado Springs, Colorado

FIlter Press, LLC • Palmer Lake, CO 80133
888-570-2663
FilterPressBooks.com

Printed in the United States of America on acid free paper.

Ghost Over Boulder Creek *is dedicated to my wise and kind husband, Rick, my creative kids, Nick and Natalie, and my office sidekick, Kiki, the little Golden Retriever.*

Special thanks to Gordon Yellowman, Cheyenne tribesman; Silvia Pettem, Boulder historian and author; my editor, Doris Baker; and my writer friends, who all greatly contributed to making this story a reality.

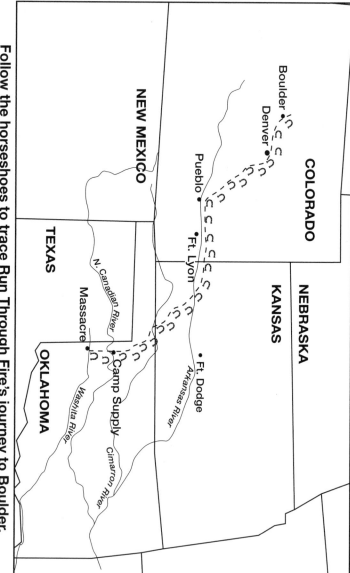

Follow the horseshoes to trace Run Through Fire's journey to Boulder.

Summer 1868

The knot of thundering buffalo kicked up a swath of dust that almost hid them from the pursuing Cheyenne boys. Arrows raced from the bows, downing several buffalo. The boys cheered as each hunter rode over to a fallen buffalo, then sat proudly atop his horse. Finally, one Cheyenne boy was left, determined to get his prey.

Run Through Fire's arm shuddered as he held the bow taut. Ready, aim...the bow string bit into his finger, as the arrow released. *Thwip!* The arrow zinged past the shaggy, galloping buffalo, straight into a cactus. A boy from his tribe rode up next to him, laughing, almost toppling from his spotted pony.

"It is the white man's blood that runs through your hands. You will never hunt like a warrior." The boy dug moccasins into his pony's ribs, leaving Run Through Fire in a dust cloud. Run Through Fire jerked his pony around and galloped in the opposite direction, away from the pointing and sneers.

Astride his horse, Chief Black Kettle called to him, his dark brown face stern. "Run Through Fire, you hunt with your head, not your heart." The early morning sun showed the lines and crags in Chief Black Kettle's face and the few white hairs weaving through his black braids. He knew so much, like the spirits themselves, it seemed. Why was it whenever Run Through Fire tried to do his best, to make his chief proud like a father, he failed?

"It was the other boys," Run Through Fire sputtered. "If not for them, I would have my buffalo." Ashamed of the words that tumbled from his lips, he looked past his beloved chief to avoid the wise gaze. He so wanted to stop the other boys' taunts and to achieve what every Cheyenne boy desires—to become a warrior.

The idea came to him as if sent by the spirits.

"I will go on a vision quest," he announced to Chief Black Kettle, unsure of what he would say next.

Chief Black Kettle thought just long enough for Run Through Fire to make his plan. "I will go to the Antelope Hills for two moons. I will wait until the spirit-being tells me what I must do to become a warrior."

Slowly Black Kettle responded, as if the words pained him, "You are not ready for this."

In shame and rage, Run Through Fire clamped his legs to his pony's ribs and they were off at a gallop, back to his tepee, his refuge from all that wounded him. He *was* ready!

In the dark of early next morning, all was silent. He tiptoed as softly as a newborn fawn. He knew how to move in silence, to use silence to capture his prey. When no eyes were upon him, he could perform great feats, like pouncing on a wild turkey. Alone, he had speared fish in the rushing creek. But when others watched—expecting, judging, hoping he would stumble—he did stumble. Today, he would prove them wrong. He would prove his chief wrong.

His pony, still asleep as he approached, squealed as he slipped the rope over its neck. They disappeared into the still-warm summer air. He had only the clothes he wore. He had no food, no water, no weapons—nothing to repel the spirit-being from coming to him.

They galloped until the sun rose and he was far enough away that it would take some time to find him. He chose a place near a stream that had long grass for his pony. The lone chokeberry bush could shade his feet, if he wished, which he didn't. Clumps of tempting berries teased him in the warming sunshine. Their fruity scent danced in front of his nose. He must not eat and must not drink. Another moon and sun must rise to give the spirit-being time to appear. Of this he was sure.

At stream's edge, he lay on his belly, waiting and listening. The hot wind picked up and scoured his throat. The stream gurgled at his ear like a happy baby. He licked his lips as they burned in the harsh sun. He had his white father's skin, always burning in the summer sun. The tribe's medicine man made him a salve of herbs to protect his skin. The other boys made fun of his pasty face when he wore the salve. It no longer mattered. He would return to the village not a boy, but a warrior, and all would be awed by his change.

He didn't know he'd fallen asleep, only that the moon had already risen, snowball bright and surrounded by stars like ice crystals. His heart hammered, and he sat up straight. The hills, flowers, rocks, and even the sparkling stream glistened in the moonlight. And then, he saw a spirit-being coming toward him. It had come! He would soon learn of his destiny, the way to become a warrior. The being moved slowly, almost crawling on its belly. As it drew near, its yellow eyes never left him, and the boy quickly felt along the ground for something sharp. The being quickened its pace, then sprang. Run Through Fire moved so swiftly he scarcely knew how he'd aimed the jagged rock between the yellow eyes. But there the coyote laid dead, not a horse's length in front of him. The rattle in the boy's heart changed from fear to joy. If only his chief and his brothers could see him now! Never again would they call him "Face Like Milk."

Before other wild animals or vultures could find the coyote, Run Through Fire buried it. The coyote must have separated from its pack. He saw no more of them the rest of the night, as he sat guard with a rock in his palm.

The coyote must have been a test from the spirit-being, he thought, as he lay down to sleep the next morning. Night was the best time to be awake and alert for either the enemy or the spirit-being to come to him. Either day or night, he would be ready.

A flash of light ripped through his closed eyelids. Half-awake, part of him knew to roll away from the streambed, curl into a ball, and avoid the lightning strike. *Kaboom!* Like a flaming arrow, the lightning shot into the chokeberry bush next to him, setting it on fire and scattering sparks. His hair stood on end. His teeth chattered. His limbs shook. Run Through Fire knew he needed shelter and had to get his pony to safety. The whites of its eyes flashed as it reared against the rope tethered to the burning bush. He untied the pony, swung onto its hot back and held on. He didn't need to urge him into a gallop.

A second lightning flash and crash sent them hurtling into the silvery darkness. He urged the pony toward the rock overhang not too far away. The lightning flashes came so often and close to the thunder cracks that he truly feared this spirit would kill him and his pony. Was this his destiny?

As swiftly and angrily as the storm spirit had arrived, it weakened and was gone. Soon it was hard to tell a fierce storm had ever blackened the sky and pelted the ground with balls of ice. Run Through Fire crawled out from under the overhang. Why had this spirit attacked him with such fury but had not revealed itself?

Now hunger punched his belly like an invisible fist. He squeezed his tired, burning eyes shut and tried to swallow but couldn't. He dragged his body up onto his pony and steered him back to the stream, willing himself not to gaze at the rain puddles along the way.

He had failed again. Why should a spirit appear to him? He was only twelve winters old and only half-Cheyenne. Who was he to think himself worthy of a spirit's guidance?

Rain puddles popped up everywhere now. And yet,

when his pony stepped through them its hooves remained dry. Laughter burst from the boy's dry mouth, crackled and unstoppable. The birds seemed to join in laughing. His pony turned its head and eyes his way, bared its long teeth, and seemed to laugh, too. What was real? What wasn't?

A memory came to him. It was the nose-burning smell of soldiers' gunpowder. It pulled him back ... back ... back ... to the Sand Creek Massacre. That was almost four winters ago. How could this be? He recoiled as he remembered seeing his people killed. He had run and run and survived with all of those who now remained in his tribe.

Now he was seated inside the tepee at a ceremony after the Sand Creek Massacre. Chief Black Kettle had proclaimed his new name Run Through Fire. "The spirits have spared your life," the chief said. "You have run with them through smoking guns and fires."

The memories faded into the heat-shimmering plain as he neared what was left of the burned chokeberry bush. The rain had snuffed out the fire, and only charred branches remained, like blackened bones. He dismounted and stared hard at the disfigured bush. Now, he had no chance for shade or food.

His vision quest was over. Twice he had been visited by danger. Still no spirit-being appeared to offer guidance. He would have to return—crawl—back to his village, like a sad dog, and listen to the jeers that would be worse than ever.

He tried to lead his pony away from the bush and toward home. The pony would not budge. Pinning his spotted ears back, it stared at the blackened bush. What was the matter with him?

"We go, now," he demanded. Still the pony stood firm.

His dry, impatient voice crackled, "We leave!"

Like a finger curling toward him, a thin wisp of smoke rose from the bush. Run Through Fire rubbed his itchy eyes and squinted in the blazing sun. The blossoming smoke column molded into a human shape.

His spirit-being had arrived.

"Did you not believe I would come?" asked the smoky form.

Run Through Fire's knees wobbled, and he fell onto them. He tried speaking, but his voice had no sound.

"There is no need for words," said the spirit-being. It seemed to smile. "I know what you seek. I have answers for you, though you may not like what you hear."

Run Through Fire fought off the sickness that churned his stomach. Why had he done this? Was he brainless as a rock, as some of his brothers had said? Chief Black Kettle had been right. He wasn't ready. He wasn't ready to hear what the spirit-being of fire had to tell him. He wanted to beg this spirit-being to leave him.

"You are called Run Through Fire for a reason. You are destined to survive not one, but two attacks upon your people. You have not fulfilled your destiny as a warrior. You will see bloodshed yet again. But survive it you must. For you will become a warrior, Run Through Fire, after you have finished your quest."

A gust of wind whipped the smoke spirit and scattered it into nothing. As if nothing strange had occurred, the pony grazed peacefully near the stream bank. Run Through Fire ran to join his pony and greedily slurped the crystal clear water from his cupped hand. He laughed again, this time with real joy in his heart. He was to become a warrior!

1 The Massacre
November 27, 1868

It was the time of the Freezing Moon. The morning star rose above the ground fog like a ghost watching from the distance. The embers in the fire ring glowed softly through the mist, all that remained of the Cheyenne celebration dance. After many weeks of eating berries and roots, the Cheyenne had seen buffalo yesterday. Now, with his belly ready to burst, Run Through Fire slept better than he had in weeks.

A loud *Pop! Pop!* splintered his sound sleep. Gunshots? In the darkened tepee, Run Through Fire bolted upright, then leapt out of the warmth of his buffalo robe. His eyes adjusted to the pre-dawn darkness, then widened with terror. *Maheó, Wise One Above, please let it not be so!*

His uncle and two other unarmed warriors fell first, shot down as they ran from their tepees. Soldiers struck down and killed mothers and children as they tried to flee. The warriors who had managed to grab bows and arrows were no match for the soldiers, who slashed the air with their sabers. The Cheyenne feared the blades more than flying bullets. The soldiers showed no mercy.

Smiling Moon grabbed her son's arm and whisked him from the tepee. A bullet whizzed by his head as they dashed through smoky darkness, away from their once-peaceful village, toward the tall grasses and ravines of the partly frozen Washita River. Amid the sounds of gunshots, women screaming, babies crying, and horses whinnying, mother and son fled along the snowy riverbank. Along the base of the cliffs, they caught up with some of their people who had managed to escape.

The brilliant morning star blazed ahead of them, as if showing the way to flee.

His heart beat like hummingbird wings. Each icy breath stung his heart. Run Through Fire slowed to scoop up one of the younger children. Breathing hard, he slid the little girl onto his back.

Just once he must look back. The warriors fought

to draw the soldiers away from the fleeing women and children. Still, there were so many soldiers and so few warriors left. The soldiers kept coming, pouring down the ridge into the village like locusts.

Run Through Fire groaned as he watched Chief Black Kettle and his wife gunned down. They fell into the ice-rimmed river, then floated away. He had loved his chief like he was his own father. Seeing his chief killed felt like a bullet tore through Run Through Fire's own heart.

"Do not look back! Keep running!" his mother yelled. She slipped on a snowy rock and sprawled in the snow, her arm turned at an odd angle. Run Through Fire set the little girl down and tried to help his mother as she lay crumpled and moaning on the embankment. It was no use. A soldier rode their way.

The soldier bound Run Through Fire's hands together, then tied the rope around Smiling Moon's waist and to the saddle horn. The soldier jerked Smiling Moon to an upright position. She staggered to her feet, never uttering a sound. With his wrists bound, Run Through Fire trudged behind his mother as they were led back to their village, still under attack.

Warriors from nearby tribes, who must have heard the

gunshots, gathered along the ridge to fight the soldiers. Hope that surged in Run Through Fire's heart soon disappeared. "Company, countermarch!" bellowed the soldiers' leader. In no time, the sheer number of soldiers advancing on the Indians along the ridge forced them to retreat.

Through burning eyes, Run Through Fire gazed upon his smoldering tepee and the charred ruins of his village. Thick smoke dimmed the rising sunlight, but he could still see the patches of red snow, bloodied by his fallen brothers. Occasional gunshots and the soldiers' whoops and hollers continued through the morning.

Nearby, one of the soldiers spoke to his yellow-haired leader. Run Through Fire had learned enough English from his white father to follow their conversation.

"Sir, except for the prisoners here, we killed all them savages. Destroyed all they own, too—teepees, animals, buffalo robes, blankets, bows, arrows, all their winter supply of meat, horses—save for the choice ones."

"Good," replied their leader. "I want a full report to General Sheridan, especially how many dead."

"General Custer, sir … a few seem to have escaped, sir."

"I'm sorry to hear that, private. Track them down. If

there are women and children, add them to the prisoners here. We can't have the newspapers calling me the savage who kills women and children." He chuckled and the private joined him with a forced laugh. General Custer stopped laughing. "But make sure you kill the rest."

Sitting in the snow, Run Through Fire thought, *If my hands were free, I would tear these white men apart.* A sour taste filled his throat as the private stepped on bodies to deliver the orders to hunt down the others. They'd find no warriors. Warriors would never have run in the first place, for it was an honor to die fighting for your people. Run Through Fire squeezed his stinging eyes shut. *I should not have run.*

2 Why Did I Live?

It was noon, the white man's word for the sun's highest point. His father had taught him this. Thin sunlight showed Run Through Fire a terrible scene. Bodies lay everywhere. Blood pounded in his temples as he took in the unmentionable things that the white men had done. He hung his head between his knees and squeezed, as if to push out the memories. *Why did I live?* Guilt filled his body like a sickness.

The stillness terrified him almost as much as the gunshots and screams earlier that morning. Fires glowed, and the smoky air clawed at his throat.

General Custer, proud as a rooster, led the soldiers guarding Run Through Fire, Smiling Moon, and the other

Cheyenne prisoners north along the Washita River. The few sad-looking ponies spared in the attack plodded along, carrying Smiling Moon and other injured. As he trudged behind, Run Through Fire whispered to Smiling Moon, "It is as if the ponies mourn as well."

A soldier riding by prodded Run Through Fire's back with his rifle. "Mouth shut!" The soldier continued to the front of the line. "Fifty-three prisoners, General Custer, sir. All women and children." Run Through Fire spotted the little girl he had carried on his back up ahead. As if she felt his stare, the little girl glanced back at him and nodded, before turning back. At least he had done something good.

When darkness fell, Run Through Fire stiffened his body against the frigid night and tried to rub his hands that were lashed together. He felt nothing in his hands or feet. In his heart, he felt only shame. His mother offered to share her red blanket. It was all she had. He pretended not to hear her and didn't reply. Why would he deserve to take his mother's blanket? He relived how he'd run like a woman along the banks of the Washita. Was that the act of a warrior? He was twelve winters old and had hunted buffalo for the first time this moon on the cold plains. *Feel the cold sink into my bones. Let icicles hang from my nose, chin, and ears. Then maybe I will suffer a little of what my brothers have suffered!*

Chief Black Kettle's words echoed in his ears. "You will be on your first warpath in twelve moons. Do not be afraid, Run Through Fire. There is no shame in dying. Nothing lives long, only the earth and the mountains." Now Run Through Fire would never know the warpath. His brothers were gone, and he was captive in a war his people never had a fair chance of winning.

Chief Black Kettle never wanted war in the first place. Just yesterday he had returned from Fort Cobb, where he'd gone to ask for protection for his people. Run Through Fire had watched him ride through the village with a victorious smile on his dark, lined face. *The chief wanted peace with the white man,* Run Through Fire thought bitterly. *The white man killed him anyway, ignoring his white flag of peace and the United States flag given to him to display. He had died honoring this flag.*

More than a winter ago, the white men had called Run Through Fire's father a horse thief and dragged him away. Chief Black Kettle took on the role of his father. The chief told Run Through Fire stories of the wisdom of his people and of the spirits—earth, rain, fire, and wind. He showed him how to hunt, how to make a bow and arrow, and how to be strong when silent. Now Run Through Fire had neither father nor chief to turn to.

He remembered that terrible, chilly June day when his father arrived in the camp in northern Colorado Territory. His father visited every full moon with Smiling Moon and Run Through Fire, and then returned to work at a ranch in a place called Boulder. Never had he missed a visit.

He could almost smell the new ink on the books and newspapers his father would bring along. He remembered the scratchy sound of pen on paper as his father made the white man's letters. His father would pull something special from his pocket for Smiling Moon—sweet-smelling soaps or a tortoise shell comb for her long black hair. But on his last visit, white men on horses had thundered into the village, put his father in handcuffs, and hauled him away. Smiling Moon said the white men claimed he had stolen the two horses he had with him. Run Through Fire knew it was a lie.

They hadn't seen his father since.

"General Custer, sir," said a soldier, startling the boy out of his sleepy memories. "Seen this boy?" The soldier gestured with his gun. "Looks more white than injun. Think he's a Cheyenne prisoner?"

"I am not Cheyenne prisoner," Run Through Fire said loudly. "I am *Tse-tsėhėsė*." Smiling Moon hissed at her son to be quiet.

The full-bearded Custer rode back down the line. His blue, deep-set eyes looked hard at the boy. "You're what?!"

Run Through Fire stiffened. "We are *Tse-tsėhėsė*."

Custer ignored the remark. "Skin's red, probably from the sun. I don't think he's Cheyenne. Hair's too light and wavy. And look at those blue eyes. When we get to Camp Supply, bring the boy to General Sheridan and me. We'll get to the bottom of this."

3 Camp Supply

The U.S. 7th Cavalry played pain-in-the-ear music at sunrise. They fired guns into the sky and flashed their sabers, as the soldiers and prisoners made their way down the hillside into Camp Supply. They had traveled all night, about forty miles to the north of the once-peaceful Cheyenne village. The ghostly moon still hung in the sky, like an ever-present bad sign.

The camp spread out along the North Canadian River in Oklahoma Territory. Behind the cut-log walls, smoke columns rose from stone chimneys and campfires. Two corners of the camp remained open, revealing log and picket buildings, tents, and the fort's headquarters. From one corner of the post, the United States flag flapped in the early morning breeze.

Smiling Moon slumped over the horse's withers, her broken arm swinging uselessly. *If only I had a travois to pull her on,* thought Run Through Fire. Other women were just as bad off or worse, though no one uttered a sound. Once inside the camp, the soldiers herded the prisoners into a tent. The Cheyenne looked at each other. Would they be shot next?

A soldier arrived with water and scraps of frozen meat to gnaw on. The proud faces turned away. The soldier snorted and threw the frozen meat to the ground. "You savages can starve to death for all I care." He looked at Run Through Fire and jerked his thumb backward. "You. Come with me." Run Through Fire sat with arms and legs crossed. The soldier dragged him to standing and rifle-butted him to start walking.

Inside General Custer's tent, the captured daughter of Chief Little Rock curled up in a big leather chair, a thick buffalo robe wrapped about her. Custer had taken a liking to her and pulled her aside from the other captives. She looked at Run Through Fire with large eyes, as if she'd done something wrong.

Custer was seated at a square wooden table. He mopped his tin plate clean with bread crust and wiped stew from his droopy, yellow moustache. The sunburn on his face stopped in a clear hat-line across his forehead. "Come in, boy. Believe you know this pretty gal, here. Monahseetah's to be my new wife. She'll have the privilege of accompanying me when we hunt down what's left of your people. She ought to be a big help in finding the campsite."

Run Through Fire didn't ask Monahseetah why she had done such a terrible thing. He knew she had no choice.

A small man entered, and Custer ordered Run Through Fire to greet the commanding officer, General Philip Sheridan. Glaring at the man, he refused to greet this stumpy-legged enemy who looked as if he walked on his knees. He never could understand how Chief Black Kettle could be so friendly with these pale, big-headed men. What had it gotten him? Death.

The boy's silence encouraged General Sheridan's fury. Spittle collected on his dark moustache as he bellowed, "You will address an officer, boy! I don't care if you were a prisoner of the Cheyenne!"

"I am not prisoner of Cheyenne. I **am** Cheyenne!" replied Run Through Fire.

"Sir," began Custer, "the boy's obviously been fooled.

Or, he could have been captured at a very early age and forgotten his beginnings."

"You may be right," replied General Sheridan. "Still, I think we keep him with the rest of them until we're sure."

"With all due respect, sir," said Custer, "if he is a captive, we might return him to his rightful folk. Not to mention we'd get the proper credit for saving a young prisoner of the Cheyenne after our successful battle at the Washita."

"I tell you, I am Cheyenne!" Run Through Fire nodded toward Monahseetah. "Ask her if you do not trust me."

All eyes were now on Monahseetah. She lowered her own and twisted her braid back and forth, something Run Through Fire had seen her do before when she seemed fearful.

"Well, girl, what is it? Is he Cheyenne, or not?" demanded Sheridan.

In Cheyenne, she finally blurted, "He is not. We … we captured him."

The interpreter translated for Sheridan and Custer, and both men nodded.

Run Through Fire's jaw dropped. Monahseetah would not look at him. Why would she lie like that, especially knowing the Cheyenne belief that once one lied, he or a family member was sure to die? Perhaps, with her father and the rest of her people gone, she didn't care if she died. Run Through Fire understood.

A muscle worked in Custer's sunken cheek as he stared at Run Through Fire. "Need to get this boy back to his rightful folk then, don't we?"

"I know the man to do it," General Sheridan said. "William Cody—Buffalo Bill. He's at Fort Lyon, in the Colorado Territory, and due to join forces with the second column when my winter campaign resumes." He turned to Custer. "Cody could make it here in a few days. Once, he rode over one hundred miles a day to deliver dispatches to me. Gave me respect for the man. I decided to appoint him Chief of Scouts for the 5th Cavalry. Cody is, by far, the best scout on the plains."

Sheridan dipped his quill in ink and scribbled on a piece of parchment. He folded and sealed it with hot candle drippings and handed it to the interpreter. "See that this gets to Cody as soon as possible." The interpreter nodded and left.

"Cody will deliver this boy safe back to Fort Lyon in Colorado Territory," Sheridan continued. "There the boy will remain until his kin is located. Meanwhile, we'll send dispatches to the military and alert the newspapers. We'll need a sketch of the boy. I want signs in all of the post offices from here to Colorado Territory."

Run Through Fire understood some of what was said. But the most important words of all—the words that rang in his ears—were *Colorado Territory*. They were taking him to the place where his father lived. This was where his people last camped, before they were pushed to the Oklahoma Territory with promises of land, buffalo, and freedom.

He thought of his mother. How could he leave her and the others? Then it dawned on him. His father could help free them. Surely, his father, a white man, could do something. Once he found his father in Boulder, he would tell him where to find the prisoners. That would be the act of a warrior. His people would respect Run Through Fire again and forget his shameful run from the Washita. This Buffalo Bill would return him to his rightful folk, all right, and help to free his people at the same time. His mouth curled upward ever so slightly.

4 Buffalo Bill

Several days passed before Buffalo Bill's arrival. Every day made Run Through Fire question this journey. Why should he be allowed freedom while his people stayed behind and suffered? The soldiers abused his mother and the other women. The young ones were hungry with little to eat but the frozen meat they'd first refused.

How could he leave them in this prison?

One afternoon, Run Through Fire was forced to sit for hours while a man sketched his picture for the white man's post offices and newspapers. After that, a soldier brought him to General Custer's tent. As he was led through the fort, he could smell fresh-cut timber. Camp Supply was new, probably built to hold the Cheyenne prisoners after the attack.

Inside the tent, Monahseetah sat in the leather chair, though she seemed more at home in it this time. Again, she looked away when she saw Run Through Fire. The tent door flapped opened, spilling sunlight across the dirt floor. A soldier poked in his head and announced the arrival of Buffalo Bill Cody.

A tall man dressed in fringed buckskin from neck to toe ducked through the opening. His presence made the tent seem smaller, just as when Chief Black Kettle entered a tepee. Run Through Fire had never seen such a large hat or thigh-high boots, which were mud-splattered but still shiny in spots.

"Ah, Mr. Cody. Pull up that chair there. You must need a rest after your long journey. Can I have one of the men bring you stew? Believe it's buffalo."

"No, thank you kindly, General Custer. Had my fill of buffalo, lately." The men chuckled. "And I prefer to stand, actually, after being in the saddle for days. I will take some venison if you have it and a whiskey." He turned to Monahseetah and looked her up and down. "What have we here, General?"

"Why, that's my new bride-to-be, Mr. Cody." Custer draped his arm around Monahseetah's slender shoulders.

"Thought she'd be a help tracking down the rest of the savages. And the boy is—well, we're not sure of his origin. But the blue eyes and his strong English suggest he's a Cheyenne captive raised among them."

"That a fact?" Cody replied, turning to Run Through Fire. Buffalo Bill cocked his head to one side as he regarded him, as though inspecting an unusual insect. Run Through Fire scowled back, more from his anger that Monahseetah was to marry this brute, Custer, and be forced to track down her own people. "Got spunk, doesn't he?" said Cody, as he finger-combed his goatee.

"If that's what you prefer to call it," said Custer. "I'd like to horsewhip him for his disrespect. Thank God he'll be off my hands soon and in General Sherman's."

"Your telegram said there'd be a handsome stipend and a newspaper story." Buffalo Bill continued to meet Run Through Fire's steely gaze.

"Of course," replied Custer, with a wave of his hand. "When the newspapers get wind of this, they'll love it. White boy captured long ago by Cheyenne, rescued by General Custer and his 7th Cavalry, is safely returned into the arms of his rightful folk by none other than Buffalo Bill." With a smug smile, Custer folded his arms across the rows of medals and brass buttons decorating his chest.

"He might be a help hunting buffalo along the way," Cody agreed. "The Fort Lyon rations have run low. With the cold weather and your winter campaign, sir, the men will need the extra meat. The boy looks to be about twelve or so. I'm sure he's already been on hunts. Am I right, boy?"

Hunt buffalo to feed soldiers? The same soldiers who would track down and slaughter the rest of his people? Run Through Fire found the idea too terrible to accept. The white men had littered the plains with the bones of thousands of buffalo. They only took the meat and left the rest to rot. The Cheyenne would never do this. It was wasteful. Every bit was eaten except the hooves and bones, and the hides were used for robes or lodges.

"I will not hunt buffalo with the man who hunts my own brothers," said Run Through Fire.

The general hit the boy across the face with the back of his hand. "How dare you address Mr. Cody with such disrespect!" seethed Custer.

The slap stung, but Run Through Fire kept his hand away from his cheek and threw back his shoulders. Never reveal anything to your enemy, Chief Black Kettle had taught him.

Buffalo Bill chuckled. "He doesn't know any better. He's been living among savages for who knows how long. What's your name, son?"

"I am called Run Through Fire."

"No, no, your Christian name," said Buffalo Bill.

With a deeper scowl, Run Through Fire pretended he didn't know what "Christian name" meant.

Custer sighed. "You've got a challenge ahead of you, Mr. Cody. Think I might choose riding down scalp-stealing red devils over this one. It might be a waste of time trying to track down his father, too."

Without thinking, Run Through Fire said, "My father we can find. He is William Tull, of Boulder, in Colorado Territory. They called him horse thief. But I know it is lie." He went on to tell them of that fateful day, June 24, 1867, when his father was taken away.

Cody snorted. "Wonderful. We're searching for a horse thief. Who knows if the scoundrel's still alive?"

"My father is not horse thief. I know he made white man in Boulder understand."

"Why haven't you heard from him then, son?" asked Cody.

"After Father taken away, the Cheyenne pushed from

reservation to reservation. He would not know *Tse-tséhése* in Oklahoma Territory on the Washita." Just as he thought he'd said too much, something caught his attention, something swirling in the dusty sunbeam behind the two men. Was it his spirit-being? Was it a ghost? Then it disappeared, with a sudden tent-rattling breeze and a moan that could have been the wind. Bumps raised on his arms.

Custer said, "Well, it's worth a try. What else am I to do with the boy? Can't return him to those savages. At daybreak, we'll move them all to Fort Dodge's prison. You'll leave at the same time for Fort Lyon. When you arrive, have someone telegraph the *Rocky Mountain News* in Denver of the boy's search for his father."

The general lit a cigar. "As soon as you've delivered him to Fort Lyon, Mr. Cody, you'll leave with the 5th Cavalry from there. Their mission is to block the hostiles from drifting westward. We'll see an end to the butchery these Indians have wrought upon the plains, upon our innocent citizens. Mark my word, this winter campaign will return peace to the frontier.

"You know, Mr. Cody," Custer continued, blowing a smoke ring that rose above Run Through Fire and Buffalo Bill, "I wouldn't ask these services of any other man.

31

The frontier will be a dangerous place after the Washita battle." He reached far back into his desk drawer, grasped a small Derringer pistol, and slipped it into Cody's hand. At Cody's protest, Custer said, "If you get caught and the Indians proceed to torture, you may want to be your own executioner. Godspeed to you."

Run Through Fire watched Buffalo Bill drop the gun into his coat pocket. That gun might be his means to escape.

5 Farewell

The bugle sounded at sunrise. A soldier came for Run Through Fire, allowing him only a hasty farewell to his mother and his people. The women and children rocked and wailed the song of loss. The morning campfire did little to warm their tired bones. Their hollow faces were ghostlike.

"My son, take my blanket," said Smiling Moon. "It is a gift to comfort and protect you from *Mĭs 'tāi*, the owl ghost."

"Mother, how will you keep warm on your journey to Fort Dodge? I have heard the journey will take a few suns. And if it is worse there than here…"

"All I need is to know you are free," Smiling Moon whispered. Again, she offered the blanket. "You will disrespect me if you do not take it." A weary smile softened her face.

Her large brown eyes appeared enormous. Her black thick hair curtained half of her face like a matted horsetail.

Run Through Fire praised the spirits that his mother's arm was healing. She cradled it in a bandana sling that a soldier had offered when no one was looking.

"I will come back for you, Mother," Run Through Fire said, as he reluctantly took her blanket. "Father and I will return to free you all. Our people will survive."

Smiling Moon touched his arm, nodding slightly. "Return to me alive, my only son."

He helped her mount the horse for the trip north. The prisoners moved out, and Run Through Fire gritted his teeth against this final loss.

"She raise you?" said a voice from behind.

With his spit-polished, knee-high boots and freshly groomed goatee and moustache, Buffalo Bill looked ready for the return ride to Fort Lyon. He belched coffee.

"My mother, yes," replied Run Through Fire, keeping his hatred of this white man hidden. No good would come from revealing his feelings. He would use this fool as his escort and then escape when the time was right.

Buffalo Bill nodded as if he understood the bond between mother and son, even if he didn't believe Smiling

Moon was his blood mother. "Got a daughter of my own. Arta. She'd be two, now. Haven't seen her for some time. She and her mother are in St. Louis." He took a deep breath. "At least they're safe there. And I aim to go see them soon."

Two saddled horses were tethered to a nearby oak tree. Buffalo Bill waved his fringed glove toward them. "Let's go."

Chief Black Kettle's horse nickered at their approach. Run Through Fire swallowed hard, wishing that any other horse had been selected for his mount. Bird Face was too good for him. Bird Face was special, considered powerful for his intelligence, with a birdlike face, sharp darting eyes, and a pointy muzzle. The horse snorted, pawed the ground, and eyed Run Through Fire as if to say, "I am yours now. Let's get out of here."

Their bellies filled with oats, the horses were restless to be off. Run Through Fire fiddled with the saddle girth, dreading the journey with this too-proud white man.

"Well, what are you waiting for? Hop on." Buffalo Bill secured a bedroll to the back of Bird Face's saddle. "We've got a lot of land to cover before nightfall. And I aim to make it back as quick as it took me to get here. Don't give me any trouble and we'll get along fine." He said it slowly, as if Run Through Fire were a small boy.

Run Through Fire cast one more glance back at his mother and others astride their horses, plodding across the cactus-dotted land. His mother's blanket and his chief's horse were now his only possessions.

The saddle felt like a boulder beneath him. He pushed against the horn, trying to find comfort. Bird Face danced under him, unhappy with a saddle lashed to its belly for the first time.

"Myself, I'd prefer to ride Brigham here bareback," said Buffalo Bill as he mounted his horse. "But it's a long ride, and we carry our provisions on the saddle back."

"A *travois*. Is better way."

Buffalo Bill chuckled. "Well, that may be, but it's too slow for me. You're in God's country now, my boy. Better get used to our ways—my ways—or you'll have a rough time of it." He clucked to his horse and Run Through Fire followed, muttering under his breath.

Soldiers nodded respectfully or waved to Buffalo Bill as he passed. The 7th Cavalry was preparing for the winter campaign against the Indians. *Clang! Clang!* resounded through the crisp air. Horses were being shod and fattened with oats for the cold and blizzards. Men grunted as they swung sacks of flour, grain, lard, and sugar onto wagons.

The air smelled of smoke and bacon. In the midst of all the labor, Monahseetah sat on the ground, awkwardly forking breakfast into her mouth.

She seemed to sense Run Through Fire's approach and looked up to nod her farewell. He returned the farewell, wondering why she was not in Custer's tent, as she had been since her capture.

"Looks like old Iron Butt may have lost his temper with your pretty Indian maiden. She'll learn."

"Iron Butt?" Run Through Fire repeated slowly.

"Let's just say it's a fond name the boys have for their general. Probably shouldn't be repeated in his presence."

Run Through Fire's eyebrow drooped in confusion.

"Nor should his other nickname ... Ringlets," Buffalo Bill added.

"Iron Butt Ringlets," Run Through Fire repeated. "Is good name for him."

Buffalo Bill laughed. "Says it all. The man can be mean as a tornado or soft as a curly-haired girl."

"I do not have worry for Monahseetah," said Run Through Fire. "She will be better than all of us."

"Probably true, as long as she's a help to Custer in tracking down your people's runaways. Soon as she stops being useful, though, and he tires of her beauty, she'll join the rest of your tribe in Fort Dodge. In the end, boy, it will be you who fares the best."

As they left the camp, Monahseetah called out in Cheyenne, "Run Through Fire, I did it for you. You are our hope! Do not forget us." Run Through Fire turned in the saddle and answered in Cheyenne, "I will be back, Monahseetah." His fist shot into the air. "I will free our people!"

He turned away from her and stared straight ahead, vaguely aware of the prairie to the right and the snow-crusted North Canadian River to the left. He was haunted by thoughts of his mother and what was left of his people. Their lives were in tatters. They were destined for prison.

As if reading his mind, Buffalo Bill said, "You'll like Fort Lyon, son. Much more hospitable than Camp Supply. Buck up! You act as if you're on your way to prison with the others. Count yourself lucky!"

*I will count coup on you soon, Buffalo Man. Then I **will** be lucky!*

Camp Supply's sounds faded into the distance as they urged their horses into a gallop. Talk was over. It was time to move on.

6 Wild Prairie

They galloped along the river until the horses tired, finally stopping to water them at a thawed pool near the bank. The winter sun provided little warmth on their faces, and Run Through Fire hugged the blanket tighter. The blanket's red and brown woven triangles reminded him of his mother and her quick smile and of the way she looked before the massacre. He should never have taken her blanket. In this cold, she'd need it. But if he hadn't, he would have disrespected her.

One long-ago evening, his father had brought meat and they had a feast, inviting everyone in the village. His mother and father sat close, but never touching. Though separated for many suns, his parents' love for each other remained clear as the stream.

A deeply buried thought surfaced. *Is my father still alive?*

A gray jackrabbit scampered out of the thicket. Run Through Fire felt for his bow and arrow, forgetting that he had none. With a quick shot, Buffalo Bill downed the rabbit. If Run Through Fire had had his bow and arrow, as he did before the massacre, he'd have killed the rabbit before Buffalo Bill had time to aim. To kill a jackrabbit brought good fortune.

"Grub tonight," Buffalo Bill said, as he dismounted to retrieve the rabbit. "We'll wait on the buffalo until we get closer to Fort Lyon. Then we can send the wagons out to bring back the meat and hides."

"The brains, innards? You bring, too?"

"Lord, no. Tongues, tenderloins sometimes, if we have room. Mostly just the hindquarters and rump. The rest we leave for the buzzards and wolves." Buffalo Bill tied the rabbit to his saddle and remounted.

"We use all buffalo," replied Run Through Fire. "Thank animal for giving of life. Never leave it."

"Like I said, you'll learn the white man's ways soon. And just so you know, I've never wasted a buffalo in my life, like the hunters coming out here from back east do. I had nothing to do with those carcasses you see lying across the prairie."

"White man kills many more buffalo than Cheyenne. Now, not many left."

"Army's strategy," Buffalo Bill said. He clucked Brigham into a trot. "Kill all of the Indians' food source. One way to defeat 'em."

A fierce wind picked up, blowing the top layer of snow from the prairie into curtains that clouded their path. The horses lowered their heads against the snowy gusts and blowing tumbleweeds, and pushed on. As the sun set, coloring the snow a shade of red, the wind finally gave up.

"Start scouting for a place to bed down," ordered Buffalo Bill.

Run Through Fire spotted a place beneath a small tree—the only tree he'd seen in miles—where the snow thinned. Buffalo Bill nodded. They rolled out their bedrolls and started a fire with dried buffalo chips, shielding it with buffalo hide so any roaming Indians wouldn't spot the firelight. Though not a roaring fire, it was enough to cook a rabbit. "When it's cooked, pull the carcass off of the stick and cut it into chunks for us," said Buffalo Bill. Arms crossed, Run Through Fire's jaw hardened as he stared into the fire.

"Did you understand my English, boy?"

"Woman work," replied Run Through Fire.

"Not when you're alone on the prairie at night without a woman in sight for a hundred miles." He gave his bowie knife to Run Through Fire and trudged through the snow with his canteen to gather creek water. Amazing! The man so easily entrusted him with a weapon. Soon he heard *chink, chink, chink* in the still twilight, as Buffalo Bill chipped away at the ice.

The jackrabbit cooked quickly, and Run Through Fire set to work awkwardly carving out pieces of meat for them to eat. When he'd finished, it looked like a wild animal had attacked the carcass. After a long swig of water, Buffalo Bill passed the canteen to Run Through Fire and let out a long belch. "I'll take my knife back, son," he said with an outstretched palm. Run Through Fire grunted, then slowly handed back the knife. He was more interested in the gun that Custer had given to Buffalo Bill anyway. He studied the man by the dancing firelight. "Who name you Buffalo Bill?"

"I was hired to feed the men laying the tracks of the Kansas Pacific railroad." Buffalo Bill gestured to his horse tied to the tree. "I had to ride Brigham through miles of Indian country to track buffalo. Over eight months, I'd killed almost 30,000 buffalo. About then, I heard this song they'd made up about me." Almost embarrassed, he started softly singing:

Buffalo Bill, Buffalo Bill
Never missed and never will
Always aims and shoots to kill
And the company pays his buffalo bill

"And you are proud of this? Proud that you do not leave enough buffalo for Indian?"

"I'm not proud of anything, boy. I just do my job. The white man is coming here by wagon or train, and the Indian can do nothing to stop him. It's called Manifest Destiny. Means the U.S. is destined to settle in all of this country."

Run Through Fire wrinkled his brow.

"In other words," Buffalo Bill added, "this continent belongs to whites. That's what the government believes. That's why the government divides your people into reservations, to protect the wagon trains moving westward.

"Besides, the government offered to teach your people farming and raising cattle. But you stubbornly refuse. We offer—"

"Not offer!" Run Through Fire screamed the words. "Push our people into Oklahoma. No buffalo to hunt there. No water. Nothing. Is barren, like Sand Creek. Our people starve. Animals starve."

"If you wouldn't attack our people and burn our homes, we might treat the Indians better," Buffalo Bill replied.

Run Through Fire leapt to his feet. Buffalo Bill grasped the rifle at his side.

"We do not harm your people until you harm our people!" Run Through Fire's breath heaved out of his chest. "Burn villages! Cheyenne turn into Dog Soldiers for revenge against whites. Not other way!"

As his hand relaxed on the rifle, Buffalo Bill slowly started to chew again, thinking over Run Through Fire's words. The fire popped and the odor of buffalo dung filled the cold, dry air. An owl flapped overhead. Run Through Fire cowered, his arms wrapping around his head, just in case the owl was the ghost of someone. Many times, he had heard stories of owls that turned out to be *sī'yŭhk,* the human ghost, tapping on the tepee flap or whistling down

44

the smoke hole. The owl dove to the ground after a mouse.

Buffalo Bill smirked. "You scared that owl's going to poop on your head?"

Run Through Fire turned fearful eyes from the owl to Buffalo Bill. Then his eyes softened at the thought of owl poop on top of his head. For the first time, he laughed.

Buffalo Bill joined in the laugh. "I'm going to tell you something. I've only killed one Indian in my life, a Sioux, when I was about your age. I worked on a wagon train, and that Indian was about to kill one of my friends. So I raised my rifle and shot. But I had no choice. That's not my calling, even if they did put in the newspapers that I was the youngest Indian slayer on the plains." He stoked the fire and yawned. "I reckon it's time for bed. Got a long ride tomorrow. We leave before daybreak."

Why had Buffalo Bill told that story? Run Through Fire wondered as he lay back. This white man was different. Maybe he wasn't like the soldiers that killed his people. Still, Run Through Fire needed to remain hardened to him, to all white men, if he was to survive. Weaving his hands together into a pillow, Run Through Fire gazed up at the canopy of stars spread across the sky. When he found the familiar, shimmering road of stars, he prayed to *Maheó*.

"*Maheó*, bring all of my dead brothers to you along the Milky Way. *E Kŭt sĭ hĭ m'mī yo.* Give them peace."

While he lay there, he listened to Buffalo Bill snore like a noisy angry wind. His thoughts turned to his mother. *Where was she? Did she see the Milky Way right now, too?*

He missed the comforting water and smoke stains that circled the top of his tepee. From his bed of buffalo robes, he had often stared at them until his eyelids grew sleep-heavy. Never again would he fall asleep while gazing at them.

Of one thing Run Through Fire was certain: His journey as a Cheyenne had ended. When the right moment arrived, he planned to be off on his own. Buffalo Bill would lead him just far enough. *Then I will escape,* he thought, *dressed as the white boy they all believe me to be.*

Far off, the owl hooted. Was it *Maheó* warning him? Run Through Fire felt a tingle, like a tiny lightning bolt, shoot down the back of his neck.

Was a ghost after him? To frighten? Or to warn of danger?

7 Billy Is Born

The world Run Through Fire had known for twelve winters was over. His spirit and soul had died along with his brothers at the Washita. To take this journey, it was time to become his other half—the white half. Being white would help him find what he needed. He wouldn't stay that way forever, he told himself, but it was necessary now. He must learn the ways of a white boy—and quickly. He knew enough English to get along and had learned some ways of the whites by watching his father. One of the best things he'd learned was spitting! Spitting was fun.

First, he needed a new name. The only English name he knew was Billy. He liked that. Billy. As his father had been called Billy as a boy, he, too, would be Billy Tull.

Before the sun cupped the horizon and splashed the sky with fire, Billy and Buffalo Bill had finished the last of the jackrabbit, saddled up, and were well on their way. They followed Beaver Creek through Oklahoma's panhandle. "No Man's Land," Buffalo Bill called it. They passed herds of Longhorn cattle being driven from Texas to the Kansas Railheads. Prairie dogs chirped and scampered among their little mounds of dirt. The two slowed their horses to a walk so they wouldn't trip over the prairie-dog holes.

Buffalo Bill headed north to cross the Cimarron River, which would lead them into Colorado Territory. He chose a part of the wide river that appeared to be frozen solid enough to cross. He told Billy to follow close behind. Tired of listening to him, Billy veered off and chose his own path. A warrior would never follow a white man.

Halfway across, Billy was thinking how to tell Buffalo Man that his name was now Billy Tull when he heard a sound like the crunch of pine needles underfoot. His heart thundered. Suddenly, Bird Face pitched backward through the splintering ice.

Hearing Bird Face's shrill whinny, Buffalo Bill whirled around. "Get off the horse!" he yelled, as he jumped off of Brigham. Bird Face screamed as his hindquarters plunged into the icy water. Panicked and grunting, the horse lunged onto the ice with its front hooves, but the ice kept breaking away. In one swift movement, Billy whipped his leg over the horse's back. As his moccasins lightly touched the ice, he felt it cracking beneath him.

He walk-slid toward Brigham, where the ice seemed stable. Buffalo Bill looped Bird Face's reins around his horse's saddle horn and urged Brigham to pull the floundering, snorting horse. Never had Billy felt so helpless as he watched Brigham try over and over to drag Bird Face out of the water.

A long stick lay on the ice, and Billy grabbed it. As Buffalo Bill tugged on his horse one more time, Billy hit Brigham's flanks. Brigham tossed his head and lurched forward, plucking the wet horse from the hole. Terrified, Bird Face danced around for a minute, shaking the cold water off again and again, as if shaking off his fear.

Billy calmed the horse and slid back into the soaked saddle. His deerskin leggings had kept him fairly dry. The hide's natural oil had repelled the water. He felt foolish and hunkered over the saddle. In his warrior quest, he had almost drowned himself and his horse.

"Make sure you stay right behind me from now on!"

Buffalo Bill snapped. Billy could only scowl at the man's fringed, buckskinned back, which would be his view for the rest of the trip.

Smoke-tinted clouds skated in from the west. Swirling snowflakes grew bigger and heavier. A buffalo herd grazed nearby with their woolly coats snow-caked, looking like ghosts on the plain. Steam plumed from their large, brown nostrils as they stared at the two riders. It seemed strange not to pursue these buffalo, as herds like this were almost as hard to find now as flowers in winter. Buffalo Bill had warned him to be patient; they'd hunt in good time.

Though he felt shame in using his mother's blanket to cover his head against the driving snow, he thanked the spirits for its warmth and for reminding him to grab the blanket before it fell into the icy water. Usually, when Cheyenne traveled in the winter, they were warmed by their buffalo robes, the hairy side turned inward for extra warmth.

"Storm's getting worse," Buffalo Bill said, after hours of silence. The silence had been fine with Billy. It had given him time to mourn his people and pray to *Maheó* to guide his mother and him to safety.

"We'll have to make better time," Buffalo Bill continued, "or we'll get stuck in the drifts. If my memory serves me,

Battle Creek should be a few hours straight ahead. Maybe the storm will have let up by then, and we'll find a sound place to ford that creek. It seems I remember that rock outcrop to your right."

Billy looked to his right but saw nothing, even as he swiped away snowflakes that dimmed his eyes. "I do not know this place," he said, shivering.

"Trust me, boy. General Sheridan didn't make me Chief of Scouts for nothing. Just keep that horse moving and don't let him stop."

Billy bowed his head against the snow and urged Bird Face faster. He felt the horse's renewed strength and was glad, after all, that he'd been given Black Kettle's smart and mighty horse.

The storm swelled, and the snow began to drift. When it rose to the horses' knees, Brigham halted. No amount of whipping or spurring could force Brigham onward. Buffalo Bill swung out of the saddle and yanked the bridle. "Come on, Brigham," he yelled. "Won't do to sit here and freeze to death. We've seen worse times than this. Come on!"

"It is *Hō ĭm ´ă hă*. He brings the snow and cold from *Nō tŭm´*, the North. I must pray to him." Billy raised his frozen hands skyward, looked up, and said, "*Hō ĭm ´ă hă*, I am in need. Help me. Stop the snow from falling, that we may live."

Buffalo Bill ignored him as he shook the heavy layer of snow from his broad-brimmed hat and resumed yanking on the bridle. The thinning snowflakes caught his attention, and he gazed skyward.

"Well, I'll be darned." His eyes seemed to hold a twinkle of respect for Billy.

Brigham could see once again and bolted out of his drift as soon as Buffalo Bill mounted him. After a while of watching tapering snowflakes, Buffalo Bill cleared his throat and said, "I know there's a good explanation for what happened back there." He laughed. "But it sure don't figure. Anyway, I'd like to thank you, boy, for what you did, whatever it was."

"Not *boy*! Name is Billy Tull. Call me Billy Tull."

Buffalo Bill chuckled. "All right, Billy Tull. Thought you'd come around and tell me who you are sooner or later." Little icicles decorated his moustache and goatee. "Billy," he repeated. "Like they called me when I was a youngster. "

"Like they called my father, William Tull. My father will be glad to see me. He works on ranch in Boulder. I have never seen."

"I'm sure. Haven't been any Indians in Boulder for several years. They've been pretty well banished. Heard it's just a town of miners hoping for that next gold rush. Tried my hand at it once, just above Boulder in Black Hawk. Never found a speck. Good thing your pa's a ranch hand. That's money you can count on."

Billy didn't understand what the white man babbled about, so he studied the weather instead. Only occasional flakes fell now. The sun peered through misty, swirling clouds. As quickly as it had arrived, the storm moved on. A coyote trotted along, his eyes narrowed searching for his next meal to emerge from some snow-buried rock or hole.

After many miles, they reached a stretch of prairie missed by the blizzard. An endless landscape of sagebrush, rock, and sand lay ahead, changed only by the occasional bluff.

The arrow pierced Buffalo Bill's hand before Billy even sensed the danger. In shock, Buffalo Bill almost toppled from his saddle. Through the haze, Billy spotted them, five or six Cheyenne Dog Soldiers atop the bluff to the right. As they drew closer, Billy recognized White Wolf from his tribe. Chief Black Kettle had tried to calm White Wolf's anger at the white men and discourage him from the warpath. By his dark and painted face, Billy guessed White

Wolf had heard about his tribe's massacre and wished revenge.

Buffalo Bill's unharmed hand went to his holster. Billy motioned for him to keep still, hoping that White Wolf would recognize him as a Cheyenne from their village.

"White Wolf," Billy called. "*Pa ha vee see va*! Good day!"

White Wolf reined in his horse and stared curiously at the boy who looked slightly Indian by the way he was dressed in buckskin and moccasins. His hair, however, hung loose and wavy. Billy had unbraided his hair in mourning for his tribe. "It is you, Run Through Fire?" White Wolf asked in Cheyenne. "You live?"

Also speaking in Cheyenne, Billy told the fierce-eyed young man of their capture and of the troops' mistaking him for a white captive. He asked him not to harm Buffalo Bill and to take his revenge elsewhere. "I know of your pain, White Wolf. But this white man will help me find my white father. He will help me free my mother, our people, from the prison. We will live on."

White Wolf flashed eyes like shards of flint toward the man who bore his arrow. The arrowhead had pierced the web of skin between thumb and finger. Blood soaked through the elbow-long glove. Buffalo Bill grasped the arrow. Eyes closed tight, he grimaced as he ripped the arrow out through his glove. He threw the arrow into the snow and turned to face the Cheyenne, his breath hard and fast.

White Wolf spat out words in Cheyenne. Billy translated: "He says he is sorry he didn't aim higher."

"You tell him he better watch his back!" Buffalo Bill seethed.

Billy hesitated. "Tell him!" Buffalo Bill said.

As calmly as he could, Billy relayed what Buffalo Bill had said.

White Wolf went for his knife, Buffalo Bill for his gun.

Billy pleaded, "Let us pass, White Wolf. Go after the soldiers who have murdered Black Kettle, our warriors, our old men, women, and children. As we make these words, the soldiers march the women and children to prison at Fort Dodge. Track the soldiers. Do to them what they have done to us."

The Dog Soldiers sat on their horses for a time—hair, feathers, and horsetails all whipping in the cold wind. Finally, White Wolf spoke. "Join us, Run Through Fire. We are your people. Show us the path of the white man. Help us to avenge our people's death."

Billy looked at the renegade band. Part of his heart wished to join his brothers. But they were a violent group, ruled by their fury rather than their minds. His quest felt right, not theirs.

"Here, our paths split as the river. Let the spirits go with you," Billy said.

White Wolf scowled, jerked his horse's bridle so that the horse spun away on its rear hooves. As the rest of the Dog Soldiers thundered after White Wolf, Buffalo Bill went for his rifle. Billy stopped him with an hand outstretched.

"No! They have let you pass. You must let them pass. There are so few of them, they will not have much chance to survive against the soldiers."

Buffalo Bill slowly lowered his rifle. "I'm only letting them go to protect you. That was my job. Otherwise, they'd all be lying all over that bluff, bleeding like I am now."

The fringed glove was thoroughly blood-soaked by the time Buffalo Bill pulled it off to examine the seeping wound. From his coat pocket he retrieved a silver flask and poured its contents over the wound. Both winced—Buffalo Bill from the pain, Billy from the alcohol odor. He'd smelled it before on the breath of visiting Indians from a nearby tribe. They'd bragged about making "good trade" with the whites—buffalo hides for alcohol. "Foolish" was the word Chief Black Kettle had used after the drunken warriors stumbled back to their village, vomiting along the way.

From his other pocket, Buffalo Bill handed Billy his red-checkered kerchief. Billy hesitated, remembering images of his bloodied people strewn across the village. Now he was helping the enemy. But this white man needed his health to guide Billy to his father. Tightening the kerchief enough to stop the bleeding, Billy asked, "Do you have chewing tobacco?"

Through pain-gritted teeth, Buffalo Bill said, "I have blood gushing out of my hand and you want to chew tobacco!"

"Our Cheyenne medicine man uses for wounds when blood comes."

Buffalo Bill grunted, dug into his coat pocket, and tossed the chewing tobacco pouch to Billy. He popped a plug into his mouth, grimaced at the bitter taste, spit-softened it, and gently pressed it to the wound. Buffalo Bill flinched, his eyes remaining on Billy as he re-tied the bandana over the tobacco plug to keep it in place. Buffalo Bill slid the blood-drenched glove back on to keep his hand from freezing as night fell.

Billy smiled. "That is enough. Wound better when sun up tomorrow."

The ghost appeared to Billy in a dream that night. Through foggy darkness, Billy was running away from something, either a gun or a saber. A faceless man waved it menacingly at him, and Billy knew he had to get away. Each time he'd choose a new path in the darkness, a snowy tree would block his escape, its black, frozen limbs growing and stretching toward him. Then the ghost appeared, beckoning him to follow. Billy ran in the opposite direction, but it always led back to the moonlit ghost, glowing in the distance.

He awoke chilled in sweat. Why was this ghost haunting him? What had he done to invite this terrifying being?

8 Buffalo

At dawn's first hint of light, Buffalo Bill sat on a rock by a crackling fire, examining his wounded hand. Billy peered over the man's shoulder to see if the tobacco plug had worked. It had. Already, the skin was less swollen and red, and the arrowhead wound was closing. Buffalo Bill turned to Billy and opened his mouth to say something. Billy gave a curt nod and poked at the frozen hardtack from last night's supper as it warmed over the fire. Buffalo Bill poured him some of the black soup he called coffee and asked him if he wanted sugar.

"Sweetwater. Yes. Is good."

"Much obliged, boy," Buffalo Bill said from behind. "The hand looks better." Again, Billy nodded. A strange feeling came over him. This healing of a white man—his lifelong enemy—was it the right thing to do?

Did he really need this white man to guide him safely to Fort Lyon? He had recognized some of this trail already and likely could make it to Fort Lyon by himself. A Cheyenne boy never loses his way. He can use rocks, watering holes, bent grass, anything as guideposts to remember a route, even years later. Maybe he should have let White Wolf finish the white man off and then made his own way.

Billy knew that without a bow and arrow, he was at the mercy of enemies, both human and beast. He eyed the pistol-shaped bulge in Buffalo Bill's pocket. Somehow, Billy would get it.

As they approached Two Butte, the final river crossing before the Colorado Territory border, a small herd of buffalo charged toward the water. Buffalo Bill gave him the go-ahead, and they took off, their horses muzzle to muzzle. Buffalo would never veer off course when heading for water, so the horses approached from the rear. Billy watched in awe as Buffalo Bill, while still riding, leaned over Brigham's neck and whisked off his bridle. The horse burst into action.

Annoyed because he didn't have his bow and arrows, Billy managed to keep up as they raced alongside the snuffling, grunting herd. The rumble of the buffalo hooves matched the beat of Billy's heart. How he loved the hunt!

"Keep to the rear!" yelled Buffalo Bill over the noise. "Don't let them break off!" Buffalo Bill was a gun's length away from a horned bull, its long beard waggling. He aimed for the lung and quickly downed the animal. Brigham galloped through the dirty haze as if he'd done it a thousand times.

When the dust settled, eleven buffalo lay scattered across the prairie. Buffalo Bill began skinning them. He tossed a knife to Billy, saying, "We'll bring in as many of the hides as we can carry to Fort Lyon. Leave the meat for the men to haul back. Should bring in about $2.50 per hide. I'll split that with you, boy, for that fine riding you did back there."

Billy's mouth fell open. His father had told him about white man's money. Never in his strangest dreams did he expect to have any. He'd only done what he'd loved to do. He had no idea what $2.50 would buy. He only knew it would get him closer to his father.

Now that they had crossed Two Butte River, the prairie seemed even more desolate. Wagon train ruts etched into the frozen earth sparked Billy's memory. This had been the route the survivors of his people had taken after the Sand Creek Massacre, exactly four winters ago. Billy was eight, and the memories returned as fresh as the wound on Buffalo Bill's hand. Of their tribe, two hundred had been cut down, mostly women and children. He saw his aunt and so many others killed, as he'd crouched next to his mother in a hole dug into a sand bluff.

He marveled that he had survived two Cheyenne massacres. Why, he wondered again, had *Maheó* spared his life and instead taken his brave chief who was a man of peace? Would his fate be much worse, maybe at the hands of a ghost?

Horse and wagon traffic increased once they were on the Santa Fe Trail. As they passed the travelers coming and going, not a head remained unturned. Here was the famous Buffalo Bill riding alongside what looked to be a white boy with flowing locks and dressed as a Cheyenne. Billy figured no one would dare question Buffalo Bill or get in the way of his business. He was right. They tipped their hats, nodded respect, and continued on their journeys.

Billy had never seen so many white men or so many wagon trains with staggering oxen, weary horses, and crying babies. People's faces were so tired, dirty, and sunburned yet had eyes that still held something—maybe hope? From as far away as Billy could see, they streamed in from the east.

Two days later, along the muddy banks of the Arkansas River, Fort Lyon loomed ahead. Buffalo Bill told him the fort was built to keep the peace and protect settlers from the Indians. Inside the stone gates, a thirty-seven-star flag flew in one corner of the fortress. To the rat-tat-tat of drums, the 5th Cavalry went through their drills. Buffalo Bill and Billy tethered their horses inside. The high-pitched scream of an axe against a grinding stone wheel ripped through the air. Behind one of the log doors, someone whistled a tune.

Buffalo Bill and Billy made their trade and brought Billy pants, shirt, boots, and a hat. The two shared a table with some soldiers for dinner. The venison and potatoes tasted good after so long on the trail with only rabbit and hardtack to eat. The soldiers stared at Billy all through the meal and made jokes about him to Buffalo Bill. Billy ignored them and shoveled in his food. But the joke that referred to Billy as "a little red nit" made him sacrifice his last bite of potato. Using spitting skills learned from his father, he blew a glob of potato across the table and into the joker's eye. *Splat!* One eye matted shut with potato spittle and the other eye bulging, the soldier jumped up, ready to punch Billy.

Buffalo Bill chuckled and caught the soldier by the coat sleeve. "Now, Captain. You know the boy's not red. He was a captive. That's why he let you have it. You would have done worse if someone joked that you were a red nit."

His face pinched with fury, the captain drew a deep breath and said to Buffalo Bill, "I suggest you get this boy some decent garments. At least his clothes will be presentable even if his manner is not!"

"Already have, sir," Buffalo Bill replied. "And thank you for your suggestion, sir."

The captain nodded curtly, glared once more at Billy, and left, followed by the others from the table.

Buffalo Bill leaned toward Billy, voice seething. "You'd better learn some manners, son, and quick! I'll not fend for you every time you make some foolhardy mistake. I won't always be by your side."

You know not how true those words are, thought Billy, as he started to plan his escape.

9 Escape

Billy felt as if he'd like to spit potatoes again, this time at Buffalo Bill for making him wear this shameful clothing. Now that he looked more like a white boy, the soldiers did treat him better. Their faces and words softened toward this "poor" boy so "mistreated" at the hands of savages.

The boots and hat imprisoned his feet and head. The shirt and pants scratched at him like bear claws. He fingered the rough cloth and examined the tight weave, so different from animal hide. He understood why the *Tse-tsêhésê* referred to the white man as *wǐ'hio* or spider, because their clothes were like spider webs.

A soldier ushered him into Major Scott Anthony's tent where he was questioned, but he offered no answers until they asked about his father.

"Have you heard of him?" Billy asked. "William Tull of Boulder, Colorado Territory." Billy waited while the commander smiled and nodded.

"Your father's not in the U.S. Army, so why should I have heard of him?" He caught Billy's gloomy expression. "Don't worry, son. The U.S. Army prides itself on tracking down any Indian tribe. I'm sure we will locate your father. It just may take some time—when the winter campaign's over, and we've hunted down every one of those Indians."

At that moment, Billy decided tonight was the night he'd leave to go in search of his father.

From his cot inside the sweat-smelly barracks, with soldiers snoring all around him, Billy watched the two guards at the fort's entrance. *Good, the night is almost moonless. But the guards are a problem.* Then Billy had an idea. Chief Black Kettle had taught him how to throw his voice when encountering a wolf. Many a coyote or wolf had turned and fled at the sound of Billy's wolf howl. This would have to be good enough to draw the soldiers outside the wall. He tiptoed from the barracks and hid behind a water trough.

Feel like a wolf, think like a wolf, now sound like a wolf.

Billy drew a deep breath and curled his hands around his mouth.

"Aoooooo!"

Even before he saw the guards look at one another and then run through the gateway to investigate, he knew it had been his best.

Quick as a shooting star, Billy was on Bird Face and galloping out of Fort Lyon. Gracefully, with its hair blowing in the freezing December night, the horse found its way by the thin moonlight as if it had run this path many times.

The Santa Fe Trail lay empty compared to the hustle-bustle of daylight. No one dared travel by night because of Indians. But Billy had changed back into his buckskin and moccasins. Much easier to survive dressed as a Cheyenne than a white boy, he reasoned, though he'd packed his white-boy's clothing in his saddlebag. The moccasins and leggings felt as soft as buffalo grease on his body. A full grin, the first in a long time, spread across his face.

All Cheyenne knew the night was a dangerous time to travel. But, if necessary, it had to be done. When Billy's eyes adjusted to the darkness, he saw a small settlement of timber and adobe buildings. Behind them were chicken coops, a cattle pasture, and rows of frozen cornstalks.

Many tracks led up to the ranch where horses dozed in the pasture. The small ranch seemed to be a stage stop. They had passed one of these before. Buffalo Bill explained the horses were used for trade with travelers whose own horses had grown too weary to continue the trail.

He continued on, following the Arkansas River along another stagecoach route northward as the Santa Fe Trail split off to the southwest. All night they traveled. Whenever Bird Face slowed to a walk, Billy dozed over his neck. From his elders he'd learned how to ride while asleep, how to get the most from a horse without running it into the ground the way the whites often did.

When he'd awaken with a start, he would quickly search the landscape for danger, then for familiar signals left by his tribe or others to mark the best trail. Piles of stones or sticks placed end to end showed the way, as did tufts of grass tied or bent in the right direction. When there was nothing, he looked for landmarks seen in his past travels—maybe a certain bluff, gully, or rock—no matter how small.

As he rode into the first town, he wondered if this was the place called Denver. Scattered homesteads and a church were all that made up the town. Denver must be farther still. Boulder would be about a day's ride beyond that.

Just before daybreak, a man left his house to milk the cows, unaware of Billy coming up the road behind him. Fearlessly, Billy called to the man and asked the way to Boulder. The man spun around. His eyes widened at the strange site of a lone Indian boy. The swinging milk pails stopped squeaking as he dropped them with a *clunk, clunk!* The man's eyes darted around, his voice croaked, "Where—where are they?"

"I am alone. Separated from tribe ... sir." He added the "sir" as an afterthought, realizing its power to keep peace with the whites.

As the man picked up his milk pails, he narrowed his eyes at Billy. "How come you speak English?"

"Father is white. He taught me. I search for him in a place called Boulder."

"This is Pueblo. Got to get to Denver first. Go about one hundred and thirty miles north to Boulder. Go through Colorado City, first, then Denver."

"Thank you, sir," Billy replied, "for help."

The man chewed on something, then spat a black glob in front of Billy's moccasin. "What might really help, boy, is if you weren't dressed looking like a scout for your tribe. You could pass for a white boy with that light brown hair and blue eyes. If you could get yourself a hat, tuck that mop of yours under it, you might save yourself from getting shot at."

"Like this?" Billy produced the small hat and tucked his hair up under it. "I have clothes, too."

The farmer probed his cheek with his tongue, suspicion clouding his face again. "Where'd you get a white boy's clothes?"

Billy told him about earning money from his buffalo-hide trade at Fort Lyon. He didn't mention Buffalo Bill in case that might alert the man to his escape. The man seemed to accept this and pointed to a nearby barn. "Get changed in there. Less chance of you being attacked by Indians on the trail than being shot by some nervous white settler protecting his family."

Billy scrambled into the barn and quickly threw on the uncomfortable white man's clothing, stuffing his feet once again into the stiff boots. But the man was probably right. The trails westward were thick with white people. White Wolf and his band had been the only Indians encountered so far. He needed to attract as little attention as possible to finish his journey.

10 Arrows and Guns

Billy's hand curved over the gun that he'd tucked inside his waistband. Buffalo Bill's gun gave him a little confidence for the long journey ahead. Again and again, he relived how skillfully he had plucked the gun from the sleeping Buffalo Bill's saddlebag. Buffalo Bill even had his injured hand draped over the saddlebag. But Billy's touch had been soft as an eagle feather, swift as a bird of prey.

Chief Black Kettle had told him, "Look closely at everything you see." Once, Billy had watched kit foxes as they first surfaced from their hole to hunt. He learned from their patience and focus before they pounced on an unsuspecting mouse. Another time, a coyote had taught him how to elude a hunter. Billy had chased down the coyote and thought he had it trapped in a ravine. But the coyote sprang past him, scrambling up some boulders and out of sight.

He congratulated himself on his own care and patience, remembering every detail of last night's escape. It kept him company over the endless white miles of ice and snow. He had felt a little sorry, even slightly guilty, about taking Buffalo Bill's pistol and leaving in the middle of the night. But what else could he do? Buffalo Bill would soon join the 5th Cavalry on their next Indian hunt, and he still had his rifle. Billy would have remained at the fort, knowing no one, waiting months for someone to track down his father.

Not that he wasn't grateful to Buffalo Bill. He had grown to respect the only white man he'd ever known besides his father. Buffalo Bill was different. He seemed to understand Indians better than most other whites did. Billy sensed the man felt a certain wonder for the natural world, not unlike the Cheyenne.

Billy was suddenly shaken from his thoughts. From behind a large outcrop of tall rocks, a small band of Indians galloped toward Billy. They looked to be Apache, not the most peaceful of Indians. Billy's hand felt the gun's shape inside his pants, but it would have been useless against them. Not to mention that he'd never shot a gun, only an arrow. Sitting as tall in the saddle as he could, Billy faced the leader, forgetting he looked like a white boy.

The band encircled him before he could draw another breath, which he hoped wouldn't be his last. The leader spoke English. "Get off horse."

"I am *Tse-tsėhėsė*," Billy hastened to say, his hands sweaty on the reins.

The Apaches looked at each other, laughed, but kept their arrows pointed toward him.

"Prove," the leader said, "before we kill you."

Billy's mind raced. He spoke in rapid Cheyenne from nerves as well as to prove he was fluent. "I have come through the Washita River Massacre. I have come through the Sand Creek Massacre. *Maheó* guides me to help our people. My path is chosen."

The Apache leader considered this a moment. "You are like a papoose out here alone, without bow and arrow. Why would the Great Spirit send you so helpless?"

Billy took a chance, going for the gun tucked in his belt. The Apaches pulled their arrows taut. The wind whipped up a small snow devil, a whirling twister of snow sparkles in the sunlight. "I have this gun," Billy said quickly. "It will protect me better than arrows. With this gun, I will kill my enemies. With each white man's death, I will count *coup* and wipe away another tear over the deaths of my Cheyenne people."

The Apache leader laughed again. "You think you alone will take on the white man? You will be dead before you become a warrior."

Another snow devil whipped up next to the other, and Billy saw this as a good sign sent from the spirits.

"But you show the courage of a warrior. Go."

With that, the arrows lowered, and the circle of Apaches split. Billy slowed his breathing as he watched them leave. He thought of the leader's words, *You will be dead before you become a warrior.* Why should that be so? He'd made it this far. *Maheó* guided him always, he was certain.

Still, a ghost had haunted his dream. And the owl-ghost had warned him. What dead person had taken the form of the owl to alert him? If only the owl had called or screeched as it appeared. Billy might have known the voice. Maybe the ghost was somebody who had been killed at the Washita Massacre. Ice cold water rushed through his veins.

When he rode into Denver, six suns had risen since his escape from Fort Lyon. He was glad that his clothing helped him blend in with the boys playing marbles on the boardwalk and running with hoops along muddy roads. Miners passed him with picks and pan-laden donkeys. Dirty, gaunt faces peered from covered wagons as the drivers loaded dry goods from the nearby store. Like Billy, they looked like new arrivals, confused and a little lost in this lively city.

Stiffly dressed gentlemen and ladies came and went, carrying nothing on their backs or in their arms. Sometimes, a man had a curved stick for walking or a woman pushed a basket on wheels with a crying baby inside. Nobody struggled under a bundle of gathered wood or animal hides. Billy couldn't imagine how many people dwelled under the big roofs of the houses he saw. He only knew that most of his tribe could live there comfortably. Tree saplings grew in the front yards carpeted with short brown grass. They must have turned horses loose on the grass to get it that short, Billy reasoned.

Behind snow-dusted windows, pine trees strung with popcorn pressed against the glass. Trees *inside* the house! Billy laughed to himself. He had heard of the whites' celebration around this time. "Christmas," Black Kettle had called it. "The whites seem to be at their most peaceful at this time," he'd explained to Billy.

It grew dark and started to snow lightly. Billy was tired and wondered if his coins were enough to get him a hot meal and shelter from the storm. The first place he wandered into had loud music and girls dancing and, again, that stomach-churning smell of the white man's water— whiskey. A man with a cigar chased him out. From the roof overhang of another building, a sign swung in the wind with crude images of a bed and a steaming bowl painted on it. This must be the whites' place to rest.

"How much for sleep and eat?" he asked the very large woman at the door.

"Fifty cents!" she barked and started to close the door.

Billy held out some coins to her, and she greedily snapped up one of them and opened the door. "Last room on the left. Get some grub in that room on the right. Still a little soup and bread left. You looking for work, boy? I got plenty for you to do around here. Those buffalo coins won't last long."

"Thank you, sir." Billy thought he'd try "sir" again since he'd seen how well it worked on the milk farmer. "But I search for my father in Boulder."

"Sir!" the woman bellowed. "If you're trying to be fresh with me, boy, I'll turn you out on your ear into the snow!"

Billy raised one eyebrow. What had he done? These whites were all crazy. It would be harder than he had thought to fit in. Quickly he said, "I am glad you offer bed and food."

The woman's voice softened slightly. "Maybe an extra coin would make me feel better." Billy dug into his pocket and gave her one more. The large woman bit into it, nodded, and led him to his room. The smell of urine wafting from a white pot on the floor almost made him sleep somewhere out in the snow. The pot hadn't been emptied since the last visitor used it. Good thing he hadn't planned to sleep in the saggy bed, since he watched a bug and mouse race each other from underneath the covers. The ground, the earth, was his bed, always would be.

Soup! Food for old men! If the other Cheyenne boys saw him now, they'd throw snowballs at him and call him "old stinking man." He slurp-gulped the soup from the bowl, leaving the spoon untouched. The soup wasn't much better than his room, though the bread was tasty. The large innkeeper eyed him from the doorway but said nothing more.

Billy lay two quilts from the bed onto the floor and sandwiched himself between them. Just as he was about to sink into exhausted sleep, he heard a flapping outside the window. He bolted up and pulled aside the window shade. A shadow winged past in the darkness. Then came his father's voice. "I did nothing wrong, Run Through Fire. Nothing wrong. Always remember."

Billy shivered, belly twisting, nose burning from the urine smell. Had his father come to him in a dream as *Mĭs 'tāi,* the owl? Or was the ghost his father?

11 Boulder

At the rooster's crow, Billy jumped out of bed ready to shake off his dream or vision—he wasn't sure which. The search for his father grew urgent; he had to make sure he was all right. What had his father's words meant? *I did nothing wrong, Run Through Fire. Nothing wrong. Always remember.* Did he mean he hadn't stolen the horses on that summer day so long ago? More important, was his father still alive?

The day dawned with Billy's frosty breath set against a sky the color of columbine flowers. His belly rumbled. The bread he'd stuffed into his pocket from the night before went quickly. With a full day's ride ahead of him, Billy let Bird Face drink his fill at the trough to gather his stamina.

The city came to life as he left the hotel. Dogs barked at him on the road. Storekeepers shoveled snow from the boardwalk. A few oxen-pulled wagon trains trudged down the main street. He hoped Boulder would not have such a feeling of being overrun by *wī'hio*. The word could mean "clever spider" or "being enclosed in something." To Billy, white people were always enclosed, whether by their scratchy clothing, their buildings, or their suspicious natures.

With the vast prairie spreading to the east and the hazy Rockies to the west, he was free. The change of scenery made his heart dance in his chest. He hadn't felt this happy since the buffalo hunt. The last time he'd seen the snow-draped Rockies was more than a winter ago when the men had taken his father back to Boulder and the army pushed the Cheyenne south into Oklahoma. The line of rocky mountains hadn't changed, never would. They seemed to welcome him back, familiar and comforting, like old friends. Billy stared at the mountains for a time, sometimes dozing in the saddle. Without his noticing, the sun had started to dip behind the mountain range.

A wagon driver's "Hya!" urging his horse up the hill crackled through the thin, dry air.

"Boulder much farther?" Billy called to the driver.

"Just up and over that there ridge, young fella," replied the driver. "Mighty fine horse you got there. Care to make a trade? Bess, here, will get you to Boulder, all right. Trustworthy steed, she is."

Billy glanced at the bony Palomino and shook his head, but he thanked the driver. The spirits themselves would have to order Billy to give up Bird Face, the swiftest and smartest horse he'd ever ridden. A pat on the withers reassured Bird Face.

From a mesa that overlooked a valley, Billy watched the day draw to a close. The misty blue-white of the Rockies sharpened into the jagged-edged, reddish, rocky slabs that walled in one side of Boulder. Snow powdered the tilting faces of the rocky slabs.

A frozen streak of water crossed the valley, watering the squares of grain and cornfields. Bordering it was a line of mostly tree stumps, cottonwoods that had been cut down to build the cabins and ranches that dotted the land.

The dusk deepened as charcoal-colored clouds and mist rolled over the rocky slabs, tossing the first snowflakes around. Billy thanked the spirits for bringing him safely to this place. He pulled up his coat collar and galloped down from the mesa into Boulder.

The wide, muddy road that ran through the heart of town seemed as good a start as any for his search. But when he passed mostly darkened buildings, he realized it would be better to search for his father in the morning.

A ranch at the end of the road seemed to draw him toward it. As he neared, the feeling came over him that he must stay there for the night. Horses roamed in the fenced pasture, and Billy slapped Bird Face on the rump and sent him on inside. One of the horses nickered at Bird Face's approach. Billy turned to see if anyone had heard. Other than the softly falling snow, nothing moved. He dashed to the nearest window. Sheltering his eyes from snowflakes, he cupped his hands and peered in. It was too dark to see anything, but he chanced it and slid open the window.

"Who's that? I got a shotgun!" yelled a man's voice.

Before Billy could turn and run he heard a soft voice. "Psssssst!" It came from a wagon behind him. For some reason, he trusted the voice and followed its sound. A curled hand beckoned urgently from beneath a blanket. "Hurry!"

He was in the wagon and under the blanket with the owner of the voice just seconds before a kerosene lantern swung their way. The *creak, creak* of snow under boots came closer, the lantern light brighter. "Where are you, thief?" a man's voice demanded. Billy's heart pounded against the floorboard. He was certain that, next to him, the stranger's heart kept beat with his own. Why was he giving Billy a hiding place? Maybe this person beside him was the thief!

The snow piled quickly, already blocking a space between the blanket and floorboard. It must have been impossible to see anything in the swelling storm because the ranch owner grunted in disgust. "Come back again and I'll put a hole through you!" he yelled into the wind, then went inside.

Slowly, Billy turned his head toward the stranger, fully expecting a pistol to be leveled at his forehead. But he never expected a girl!

"You girl!"

"And you boy! Now that we've got that straight, let's get out of here before Pa comes back." The way she slithered from the wagon impressed Billy. First one leg, then the other, then her whole body rippled over the wagon's side like a waterfall. In a moment, they'd heaved themselves through an open window on the other side of the house and into the girl's bedroom. She turned up the lamp and shook snow from her long pigtails.

"All right, who are you? And why are you trying to break in our house?" she demanded in a hissing whisper.

Nerves shaken, he blurted, "I am Run Through Fire—I mean, I am Billy!"

"Well, which is it?" She looked him over. "Why, you're … you're *injun*, ain't you?" Her eyes widened with fear and fascination.

Billy wasn't sure whether he should confess to this girl or not. Finally, he said, "One part. Other part, white, from father."

"My Pa would call him a squaw man."

"What?"

The girl pursed her lips, frustrated. "Your ma's a squaw, right?"

"Her name Smiling Moon," he replied, lifting his square chin.

"Pretty. I bet she fits her name. My mama fit her name—Rose. She's in heaven, now, with my baby brother. He never got no name."

Billy said nothing, felt nothing. To him, this girl losing her mother and brother was tumbleweed in the wind, a hair falling from his head.

She looked at him sharply. "What's your business here?"

"I need shelter. Sun up, I look for father."

"You think you can just break into someone's home to sleep? You'll get killed long before you find your pa."

"It is cold. I have no shelter."

"Going to have to use the barn then. Wouldn't be proper for you to sleep in my room, and anywhere else in the house is too dangerous. I'll fetch you some grub. By the looks of it, you need it. I can almost see through you, Run Through Fire. Ha! Maybe they should have named you Run Through Me!" She swallowed a giggle when Run Through Fire didn't crack a smile.

"Do not say Indian name. I am Billy."

"Smart, if you plan to stay alive in this town." She brightened. "Sorry to be so rude. I'm Rebecca Conner. How about some dried cherry pie? It was my mama's recipe, and she's a prize winner!"

"Eat dried cherries, yes. What is pie?"

She ran a tongue over her upper lip, almost touching all of the little spots below her nose. Little brown spots ran all over her neck and face and up to her red hairline. Billy figured she was near his age.

"Mmmm, mmmm!" was all she said before leaving him in her room. She returned almost as quickly as she'd left and held out a crumbly wedge of pie in a red-checkered kerchief.

"You're in for a treat," she said, nodding for him to dig in. After a quick sniff, Billy nibbled off a small bite. Then he gobbled it all in one more bite, even licked the kerchief clean.

"*E-pevaʔe*. It is good. More," he said, thrusting the kerchief at Rebecca.

"For someone who's been caught trespassing, and being an injun to boot, you're pretty bold," she said. "Anyway, that's the last of it. I'll sneak you breakfast tomorrow. So go on, now. I got chores early. Out the window with you. And be quieter this time."

He cocked his head to one side. "Why you not tell father?"

"I watched you the whole time when you put your horse in our corral. Then, when you snuck around to my pa's bedroom, I figured by your size you were a boy and couldn't cause too much harm. Guess I took a chance. No one's ever called me a fraidy cat." She shrugged her skinny shoulders. "Looks like I was right."

Billy didn't move. Rebecca shifted uneasily. "That blanket of yours ain't going to be enough. Here's a quilt. It's my extra quilt Mama made especially for nights like tonight, before typhoid fever got her and my baby brother."

Either to stop the tears from spilling or to make a fierce expression, she wrinkled her freckled nose. "So you take care with this. I find even a speck of horse poop on it in the morning, and you'll be a scalped injun! Understand?"

Billy nodded and then climbed out of the window with the quilt under his arm. Before she shut the window, he turned to say, "*Há-ho*. Thank you, sir."

The girl with a body as narrow as a tepee pole smiled, then pulled down her window shade.

12 Morning on the Ranch

The quilt and a pile of straw was not enough to keep Billy warm, but it kept him from freezing. At dawn's first milky light through snow-burdened clouds, Billy walked with numb feet back to the ranch house and the strange girl with hair of fire.

He passed Bird Face, who looked miserable in the pelting snow, standing apart from the white man's horses as if he knew he didn't belong. Billy apologized to the horse for taking his barn space, but Bird Face could better weather the storm.

Billy crept into Rebecca's room and stood by her dresser. She awoke with a start. Looking half-pleased and half-scared, she asked him in a whisper if he'd slept all right.

"Cold."

She nodded. "I thought I'd dreamed you."

"I am hungry."

"Breakfast ain't even cooked yet. Chores have to be done first. You'll just have to wait, Billy."

He nodded. "I not here to do bad thing. Father here in Boulder."

"Can I help you find him?" Rebecca asked, yanking off her nightcap. " 'Bout four hundred folks in town now. I know a lot of them. I've been here almost as long as there's been a town. I was born on our way out here in '57, dead smack between Illinois and here. Eighteen of us, five wagons, and eleven horses. Took six weeks, my pa told me."

She poured water from a pitcher into a bowl, then splashed it on her face and toweled it dry. "All log cabins, back then, dirt floors, no windows," Rebecca continued. "Pa said they had a dance in one of them cabins that first Christmas Eve. Now we hold our dances in the schoolhouse. Got sawmills now. Hear them? It's a good place to live. If your pa's a smart one, he'll have stuck around. So, can I help?"

This girl, Rebecca, had so many words. He waited for her to catch her breath, and when she didn't, he took a deep breath himself. "No help. I will do it alone."

Rebecca pulled out a woolen dress to wear and muddy boots. She spun her finger in a circle, indicating he should turn his back. After he had done so, she said, "Oh no, you don't need help. So far you've only had to eat our food and sleep with our horses."

Hastily she buttoned the last button as he turned to answer. "I need no one's help. I go now."

"Don't be foolish. You need food. Where will you go?"

"I must find my father."

"Listen, I have a masterfully good idea!"

Billy didn't know what *masterfully* meant, but the gleam in her eye told him it must be something good.

"I'll introduce you to my pa. I'll tell him something like, 'He just showed up this morning looking for work. Since we haven't had a ranch hand here in over a year, how 'bout hiring this young fella?' "

"I know things about this," Billy said. "My father ranch hand."

"Don't that beat all? What's his name? Maybe I've heard of him."

"Rebecca Sarah Conner!" yelled a raspy male voice. "Whose horse is in our pasture?"

"That's Pa. Come on. Just nod to everything I say."

90

Billy followed her as she found her pa outside the pasture gate, hands on his hips. "Who's this?" he barked.

"Name's Billy, Pa. He's looking for work. We could use another ranch hand, Pa. With Mama gone, I can't keep up with all of the house and the ranch chores. He rode up here this morning, and I told him he could put his horse in our pasture while we asked you."

"Where's your folks, boy?" demanded the tall, lanky rancher.

"My father in Boulder. I look for him."

"And looking for work, too? Don't make sense," replied Mr. Conner.

What would sound believable? Billy thought. "I must eat," he said simply.

"Pa," said Rebecca, "couldn't we let him do some odd chores around the ranch, earn his keep, until he finds his pappy? He might be prospecting in the hills, for all we know. You know what happens to those men up there. Sometimes folks don't see them for months. Then they hit gold!"

Mr. Conner pushed back his hat and scratched hair that was almost the same color as his daughter's. "Prospectin's for fools. Been nine years. It's played out. Ain't no more gold, I'd wager." He stroked his bearded chin. "Suppose I could give you a try. Got a section of fence needs mending."

Lines deepened around his narrowed green eyes. "Say, that didn't happen to be you last night, trying to break in?"

"No, sir!"

"Uh, maybe it was a coon, Pa?" Rebecca said.

"Humph! Raccoon's are getting smarter than the president, these days. Take that raccoon that broke into the neighbor's house the other night. Got into all their preserves and no one heard a sound. Knew it was a raccoon, though. Know how?" He chuckled. "Strawberry jam coon tracks!" He laughed again and told Billy to follow him over to the broken fence. Billy glanced back at Rebecca. She winked at him. Was this a good thing? Though he returned the wink, it seemed more like something you did with a bug in your eye.

After working on the fence, Billy and Mr. Conner went inside for breakfast. The only foods Billy would touch were the apple preserves, which Rebecca proudly announced came from their apple trees, and the flapjacks, which reminded Billy of the cornmeal cakes his mother made. The pork sausages smelled strange to him, strong and unpleasant.

"Kind of picky, ain't you?" commented Mr. Conner. "Think you'd be starving after the work you did on that fence. Never seen any boy turn his nose up at pork sausages. Have you, daughter?"

"That's all right, Pa. All the more for those who do eat it, you always say."

"That I do, girl," Mr. Conner said, while forking himself two more sausages and sliding them onto his plate. "Now, what business is your pa in, boy?"

"Help on ranch," said Billy. "Work with horses."

Horace Conner stopped in mid-chew, forced down the mouthful and growled his next question. "What's your pa's name?" He took another bite, eyes on his plate.

"Tull. William Tull. Have you—?"

Billy ducked, narrowly missing Mr. Conner's sausage spewing across the table.

Horace Conner composed himself, dabbed at the corner of his thin lips, and sat back in his chair. He stared at Billy. At the end of the table, Rebecca fared worse. Her knocked-over hot cocoa darkened the checkered tablecloth and dripped down the side of the table to the rag rug below. She didn't bother to right her mug as she sat back against her chair. She, too, stared at Billy.

Finally, Mr. Conner said, "You're—you're William Tull's son?"

Billy felt sick. "What is wrong? Tell me!"

Rebecca looked to her father. He shot her a look that would have sent a wolf yelping away.

"He's gone," Mr. Conner snapped, then drained the last of his coffee, as if his explanation was enough.

"Where is he?" demanded Billy.

"I want you out of my house!" snapped Mr. Conner. "Why, you're probably spying for your people. Just like your pa. You've got until sundown to get out of town." He threw his tin plate and mug into the dry sink and slammed the door behind him as he left the kitchen.

Billy turned to Rebecca. Tears pooled in her blue eyes. She shook her head and ran from the room.

13 The Deserted Cabin

"You must tell me where my father is?" demanded Billy, after cornering Rebecca in her bedroom.

She slung her knapsack over her shoulder and swiped away the last tear. "Leave me be. I have to get to school."

Arms folded across his chest, chin raised, he didn't budge from the doorway. "Tell now!"

"Please, let me by, Billy, before Pa gets back. There'll be trouble if he finds you still here."

"I do not fear him."

"Well I do! Listen, if you let me by now, I promise I'll tell you everything. Meet me after school by the big blue spruce. Listen for the ringing bell. Then follow its sound."

"You will tell everything?"

"Cross my heart and hope to spit!"

He cast her a curious look but stepped aside. She bolted past him. "Remember, stay away from Pa."

He watched her run down the road. Horace Conner ambled toward the house from the cow pasture. If Billy didn't hurry, he'd be trapped inside the house with the rancher. No telling what this white man was capable of, judging by his daughter's fear of him.

Billy ran out the back door, across the horse pasture, and quickly bridled Bird Face. As he mounted him, he heard Horace Conner's gruff voice. "Thought I told you to get the heck out of here!"

From the back porch, Horace raised his rifle and took aim. A bullet zinged by as Bird Face galloped through the open gate. Billy knew from watching his elders to swing under the horse's neck and hang there, his feet hooked around the horse's withers. It never occurred to him to shoot back. The precious bullets must be saved for a time he'd really need them.

Down the road and out of danger, he slowed Bird Face to a stop. He dropped from his neck, took hold of the reins, and led him to a nearby stream, a narrow ribbon of sparkling water threading through snowdrifts. The horse drank and grazed on tufts of dried grass. Cross-legged, Billy sat on the bank and thought.

Much had happened since his arrival, none of it good. Something bad had happened to his father. The white man, Horace Conner, was somehow involved. Why else would he be so eager to drive Billy out of his home and this town?

A wet muzzle brushed against his ear and playfully pushed him over into the stream. Splash! The frigid water rushed over him, but it wasn't deep yet, as it would be when the spring snowmelt gushed down the canyon creek into the valley. His laugh escaped through chattering teeth. "All right, little Bird Face! You are telling me I stink like the skunk. I will bathe."

Vigorously, he rubbed the icy water over his body. It was agonizing and wonderful at the same time. Along with other young boys, he'd been taught how to bathe in wintertime. This was easy compared to the more vigorous tests a Cheyenne boy must face. When the scorching sun peaked, he would run for a long time. At night, he'd remain awake and alert. The next day, a sweat lodge would force the water from his body like a waterfall. The whole time, he drank nothing, ate nothing. All of this and more

Billy had endured to be a warrior someday. It had made him strong and able to withstand this journey to find his father and help his people.

The puddles inside his boots squished as he climbed the bank. He pulled them off and dumped out the water, feet reddened and wrinkled like old apples. In the satchel, he found the comforting, bright yellow leggings that distinguished his Cheyenne people from other tribes. The moccasins, with their vertical lines of beads, felt like warm animal grease. "Ahh" escaped from his lips. He wrapped the blanket about him, wrung out the white boy's clothes, and spread them on a bush to dry.

There weren't many places for a Cheyenne boy to hide for long in this snowy valley, scattered with tree stumps and cabins. Patches of plowed-over fields spread across the land. Cattle and horses nibbled at yellow grass that pushed through the snow. To avoid being seen, Billy and Bird Face galloped past all of this until they reached the mouth of the canyon. Through a thicket of pine near the creek they stumbled upon a cabin that looked deserted. Billy took a chance.

The dirt floor still had boot prints, but the snow-covered mattress looked unused. Shards of sunlight cut across the windowless cabin, pointing to cracks wide enough to allow snow to blow in onto the bed. Dim light revealed things left behind: rusted tins of food, a water basin and bucket, snow-covered miner's clothes, and a few mining tools.

He recognized the divining rod and miner's hat with a candle still fastened to the front. Once, his people had come across an abandoned mine shaft, and Black Kettle had explained what the leftover items were used for. A miner held the divining rod—a forked stick—over a promising piece of land in hopes that it would lead the seeker to gold or silver. The candle in the miner's hat was lit just before the miner was lowered in his cage to the mines below.

Maybe whoever had lived here gave up ever finding a claim and moved on.

Billy held the clothes up to him. Not bad. If he tucked the overalls into the boots, like he'd seen white men wear them, and rolled up the shirtsleeves, it might work. The boots, on the other hand, were as big as canoes.

If he kept his feet clamped to Bird Face's belly and never dismounted, no one would notice. At least the stiff boots would keep his feet warm until the others dried.

He tried walking—or shuffling—to the door, then out into the snow. The snow seemed to grab his oversized boots like a monstrous white glove. Billy toppled out of the boots, face-first into a drift. "Argh!" Bird Face nickered his appreciation.

Snow covered his face. Billy spit out a mouthful and playfully said to the horse, "Again you laugh at me!" He plucked the boots from the snow and practiced walking.

Now he needed to start a fire to dry his other clothes. Wood was scarce. While searching for it, he found a sled propped against the back of the cabin. Maybe it had been used to carry goods from town. Billy had spotted some boys in Denver riding a sled down a hill. With other Cheyenne boys, he'd coasted on big strips of bark, standing on one end and holding the other end with a strip of rawhide. But the white boys rode on their bellies. Fast. *I go faster*, he thought.

The trail along the creek was just steep enough to get some speed. "*Wah! Wah!*" burst from his lips as he sledded down the trail. He tumbled off the sled just before it crashed into a pine tree. From the top of the hill, Bird Face once again nickered.

"Fun," Billy said, out of breath. "I do this again."

He collected enough tinder to start a fire in the small fireplace. Billy made a fire-stick by splitting the end of a stick with a knife. Then he inserted a piece of hardwood, sharpened to a point, into the split and lashed the two together. He rolled the stick between his palms. The end of the stick spun and ground on another piece of wood, finally made a glowing coal. He dropped it into the tinder. Patiently, Billy blew on the coal. The tinder burst into flames, and he laid the wet clothes nearby to dry.

Billy danced around the fire in the small cabin and sang ceremonial songs until he collapsed with exhaustion. Suddenly, he heard the peal of bells. Rebecca! How long had he been in this smoky cabin, dancing in a dreamlike state the way he used to do during ceremony? As fast as his new big boots would go, he tore out of the cabin, smoke rushing out after him like a gray ghost.

Boy and horse raced down into town, following the creek. Wagon and buggy tracks had tamped down the snow in the wide road, making travel easier. People stopped along the boardwalk to stare at the commotion.

He galloped past a hotel and a hardware store with windows decorated with greenery and red bows. The bells had stopped. Billy hoped he wasn't too late to meet Rebecca.

14 The Ghost Over Boulder Creek

Surely the bells came from this direction? He could recognize a mountain lion's prowl at night. Why couldn't he track the school bell? Finally, he spotted the tiny, white-frame schoolhouse. Stomping her boots and rubbing her arms against the cold, Rebecca hunkered under a big spruce.

"About time!" she called.

"I found cabin in canyon. Good place to stay."

"Sounds like old Mr. Murphy's cabin. He died in there. Never did find a lick of gold."

Billy swallowed hard, partly from the fear of staying in a cabin where a man had died, partly from his smoke-raw throat. "Now, tell about my father."

"I need to take you somewhere first," she said, her brows pulling together.

"You ride behind me on Bird Face."

As they followed Boulder Creek upstream, Rebecca steered them back toward the center of town. One lone cottonwood beside the creek bed bounced its branches in the chill wind. It wasn't the wind that froze Billy's heart. There was something about that tree.

And then Rebecca told him to stop. Why, why at this tree? Curiosity rooted him to this spot. Fear urged him to push on. For a long time, Rebecca stared at the tree, sniffing away what sounded like tears. Finally, she said, "This is the place."

"What place is this?" Billy asked, shifting uneasily in the saddle. Bird Face spooked for no reason, shying and backing away as if a snake nipped at his hooves.

Breathing fast, Rebecca gestured toward the cottonwood. "That's where … where they hanged your Pa."

Billy jumped from the horse and staggered backward, his glassy blue eyes flitting from the tree to the girl, then back to the tree. "*Ah hey!* It cannot be so!"

"I'm sorry, Billy. Really. But you had to know."

"When?" was all he could say.

"About a year and a half ago. A posse dragged him into town and kept him above Dabney's Blacksmith Shop. We got no jail, you see. They thought he was a thief and an Indian spy and—"

"Not thief! Or spy!"

"He was supposed to bring the two horses back and when he didn't, Pa thought—"

Her voice trailed off, the coloring beneath her freckles went pink.

"Your father did this?"

Almost in a whisper, she said, "They were his horses."

"My father work for your father?"

She nodded.

"Tell more," he commanded, trying to keep his anger and grief in check.

She drew a shaky breath. "Sometime during the night, a mob took him from the blacksmith shop and then … and then … they hanged him." She looked off into the distance. "They buried him on Lover's Hill, near the bottom where they bury poor folks. A lot of the town folk were against the hanging. Pa said it was the right thing to do, since Mr. Tull stole the horses from him and was probably a spy for the injuns."

"My father never spoke of whites. Came only to see my mother and me. He was a good man. He not take horses!"

"There's one other thing, Billy." She looked hard at the ground, as if trying to figure how to say something. "They've seen his ghost!"

"Ghost?"

"Your pa's! Right here! I hear he carries his rope and—"

"Who has seen this?"

"First time it was the judge riding with another fellow. Another time it was Deputy Sheriff Russell. He rode along the creek one day and saw it plain as my pigtails. Broad daylight. Ain't ghosts partial to the dark? I always thought so. But the deputy swears it was a ghost. Even said his horse got spooked."

"My father's spirit is here," Billy said.

Startled, Rebecca said, "Where? You see him, too?"

He shook his head. "I must return. Alone."

She shivered. "Fine with me! Just talking about it, here, feels like any moment my pigtails are going to stand straight up. Let's get out of here, huh? Pa will take a belt to me if I don't show up soon."

Moving like a stiff, old man, Billy mounted Bird Face who was wild-eyed and raring to go. This was the last place his father had been alive. He wanted to see him again. But could he face his father's ghost? Even the bravest warriors he knew were afraid of ghosts.

Billy went the long way on the back roads to avoid the stares. "Folks are sure to tell Pa they seen me riding alone with a fella. Pa will figure it was you and hunt you down."

"I would be glad of this," Billy said loudly. "He had my father killed!"

"I liked your pa, Billy," Rebecca said softly, behind him in the saddle. "He was a hard worker. Know what he used to call me? Orange Head!"

"Good name for you."

Rebecca put on a false frown. "Watch it, fella! I'm the only friend you got." Then she smiled. "I didn't mind because he'd be extra kind to me after Pa would whip me for something. Even made me a doll once, out of cornhusks. I thanked him, but I got no use for dolls. Funny thing—he never mentioned he had a family."

"My father thought it best white men not know of his family. Not want them to come to *Tse-tséhésè* camp. Still, they track him down."

Softly, Rebecca said, "But the horses didn't belong to him, Billy."

Billy stiffened. "My father say horses were his. I believed him."

He took her as far as he could and then let her off, halfway to her house. If she hurried, she wouldn't be too late.

Briefly, she trotted backward and called, "You can always come see me when the school bell rings, Billy! I'll keep your secret safe."

Rebecca Conner was right. She was his only friend.

15 The Cemetery

Billy gritted his teeth to stop the tears and headed back to the cabin to pray to *Maheó* for guidance. He was used to being alone, but he had never felt alone or lonely. Now he felt both, like being lost in a dark cave.

His father was dead.

How could he help his people?

And if it were true, that his father's spirit had appeared, would Billy see it, too? He wanted to see his father once more. But did he dare? Did he have the courage to view his father's ghost? He'd heard stories of spirits lingering to take children with them. Was that his father's wish?

Up ahead, a small cemetery unfolded down the gentle slope, eleven or twelve gravestones, at most. Near the bottom picket fence were only two graves. Rebecca's words came to mind. *They buried your pa at the bottom of the hill in the poor section.* After tying Bird Face to the swaying, creaking fence, Billy carefully picked his way down the hill of gravestones and little wooden crosses. Snow blocked some of the gravestones, but one little cross caught his eye, one word scratched into the center.

Tull

A cold wind whipped his hair across his face. The anger that steeled his jaw turned to fright as he pushed the hair out of his eyes. What was happening? What was this feeling?

On the other side of the grave appeared the ghost of his father.

The ghost floated, shimmering white against the snow. So white it was hard to tell it was his father, but for the telltale beard and large blue eyes.

"It is you, Father?" Billy whispered.

In one hand, the ghost held a long rope. The other hand extended toward the boy. Billy yearned to take hold of his father's hand, but what if the ghost whisked him off into the ghost world? Still, to touch a ghost—and that of his own father's…! His trembling hand went to meet his father's hand, but the ghost pulled away and pointed to the north.

"What is it, Father? What are you showing me?"

The ghost opened its mouth to speak, straining for words. Nothing came, only the moans of a knife-sharp wind. The picket fence creaked and swayed. Snow crystals blew off a nearby pine tree and floated through the air.

Again, the ghost pointed a bloodless finger toward the north, cocking its head in the same direction. Behind Billy, Bird Face let out a shrill whinny, reared, and broke the reins that tied him to the fence. He took off at a gallop down the hill. Billy was only barely aware of the horse. He was afraid to turn away, afraid the ghost might disappear before Billy learned of its wishes. What if the ghost never returned?

Bird Face didn't get too far away. The ghost chased the horse, skimmed onto his back, and reined him around. Bird Face bucked and reared all the way back to the cemetery, thoroughly unhappy. The commotion drew an old man from his log cabin down below, shotgun in one hand, the other fist shaking. The ghost vanished.

"What in tarnation you doing up there, boy? You doing something to those gravestones? I catch you here again, you'll have a bullet in you and your horse!" The old man pointed the shotgun into the sky and fired. Billy grabbed Bird Face and jumped on. They took off at a gallop and soon disappeared from the old man's view.

Billy slowed his horse to a walk and thought about his father. William Tull had died young, a white man who had lived partly in the Cheyenne's world but mostly in the white man's world. In the end, he'd been betrayed by his own race. But he had died a noble and good man. Billy was proud to be his son.

Today Billy had proven himself a warrior. He'd done what most warriors, even the Dog Soldiers, were too fearful to do. He had faced a ghost and spoken to it. He must find out what his father had tried to tell him, maybe something important that could clear his name. That old man's threat made returning to the cemetery out of the question. The cottonwood tree would be a better place to see his father again. Now, he'd wait for darkness.

16 Arrested!

The deer never knew Billy was near, as he aimed and shot his gun for the first time. How easy it turned out to be, though he preferred the quiet of his arrow to the gunshot noise. He thanked the animal for giving its life that he might live. With the deer slung across Bird Face, they continued the rest of the way toward the cabin. He would hang the deer carcass for drying. Then he'd use the knife he'd found in the miner's toolbox to cut up the meat.

Bird Face whinnied. Another horse returned the whinny from behind pine trees in the twilight. Before he knew it, two men on horses blocked the trail.

"That's him, all right," said one man.

"What's your name, boy?" demanded the other.

"Billy."

"Billy what?"

"Billy Tull, sir."

The two men looked at each other, and then the skinnier, younger one unrolled a piece of paper. He leaned over, showed it to the older one, and said, "See, Sheriff. Says here, 'Called himself Run Through Fire upon his capture … believed to be a white boy, captured long ago by the Cheyenne and wishes to make contact with his father.' " He poked the paper hard for emphasis as he said, "William Tull!"

"My father is dead!" Billy snarled.

"You bet he is," replied the sheriff, with a snort. "I tossed the hanging rope onto his coffin when we buried him. Sorry to say, boy, but your pa was a horse thief."

Billy went for his gun. The deputy swung the butt of his rifle, knocking Billy off of his horse. The last thing he remembered was cold snow cradling his fall as he tumbled to the ground.

The smell of Bird Face's sweat and dust filled the boy's nostrils as his head bobbed against the horse's belly. He thought he was traveling the open prairie again, though his head throbbed and he tasted blood in his mouth. His eyes flew open at the two sets of hoofbeats next to him. He tried raising his head, but pain shot through his jaw like the claw of an eagle. Then they stopped and Billy heard, "You found him." He recognized Horace Conner's raspy voice.

Somebody pulled him from the horse. He pretended to be knocked out as he was carried up squeaky wooden stairs. He was bounced onto a bed that smelled of human sweat. The bedsprings dug hard into his back. He opened his eyes.

"Shouldn't have gone for your gun," the skinny one said, with a rotten-toothed grin.

The sheriff came in with a small snowball in his gloved hand. He gave it to Billy. "Put this against your jaw. Ought to bring the swelling down."

"Was he up at Old Man Murphy's place?" Horace Conner wanted to know as he lit a cigar.

"Just returning," the sheriff said. "By the looks of it, the boy was planning to stay there and make it his home. Isn't that right, boy?"

"No one live there," Billy replied. "I saw no harm. I need shelter."

"I saw the smoke coming from there earlier on in the day," Horace said. "Had a feeling the boy might be up there, even though I told him to hit the road. You broke the law, boy, just like your pa. You busted into my home. And now you've trespassed on private property. So, welcome to our jail. The same one your pa stayed in."

Though he rose to his elbows to answer Horace Conner, the pain was too great and he lay back down. "My father did not break law. You had no right to hang him!"

The deputy cackled, shooting spittle through gaps in his teeth. "Feisty, ain't he?"

"We had every right, boy," the sheriff said, lighting a cigar off of the one Horace Conner was smoking. "Horace swore out a warrant for his arrest after he took off with the two horses. And we didn't want no Indian spy living among us. So we killed two birds with one rope."

The deputy cackled again, joined by Horace Conner.

Billy spat on the sheriff's boot.

"That'll cost you," said the sheriff. He grabbed the handcuffs clamped to the iron bedpost and shut them around Billy's wrist. The sheriff tossed the skeleton key into the desk drawer.

Billy didn't even try to fight. What was the use? The white men had won.

17 Orange Head to the Rescue

Clang! Clang! Must be Camp Supply. That familiar iron-on-iron sound woke him every morning when he was there, as the blacksmith began shoeing his first string of army horses. Billy cracked his eyelids open. This wasn't Camp Supply. Now he remembered. The handcuffs, which had bitten into his wrist as he tried to sleep, brought it all back. He was above Dabney's Blacksmith Shop, in Boulder's makeshift jail, held for no reason other than he was the son of William Tull.

The door creaked open and a burst of white morning light and snow streamed across the floorboards. Rolling to his side, Billy braced himself for what was to come. Hanged from the same cottonwood as his father, he suspected.

But to his surprise, it was Rebecca Conner. Just like the first night he had met her, here she was again, coming to his rescue. She slipped in, closed the door, and hurried to his side. "Billy!"

"Orange Head? How—"

She put a freckled finger to her lips. "Guard outside's asleep. Pa told me this morning how they'd caught you. Said they're going to send you back to Fort Lyon. They've already sent a telegram."

"Key there," Billy said, pointing to the desk. A gun lay next to the key.

"And this little toy here, might this be yours?" Rebecca asked smiling. Buffalo Bill's pistol dangled from her finger.

Half of Billy's lip curled into a smile. "These *wī' hio*— not very smart."

She unlocked the handcuffs, and they hurried out the door. Billy rubbed his aching jaw. They stopped at the top of the stairs. The deputy snored in a chair at the bottom, rifle across his chest.

"He smells like whiskey, so I think he's sleeping it off. But be careful," Rebecca whispered. She tiptoed down the stairs. Billy followed.

Like an orange cat, she slipped past the deputy with

only inches to spare between them. Now it was Billy's turn. No problem for a Cheyenne warrior like himself. He was almost past the guard when Bird Face noticed Billy and nickered to him. The guard's chin slowly came off of his chest. His reddened eyes squinted open. He blinked away the dazzling snow light and tried focusing on the source of the noise. Then he aimed the shotgun toward the fleeing pair and fired.

The deputy's aim hit a tree branch, knocking off a mound of snow. The shotgun blast sent him backward over his chair. By the time he'd scrambled out of a snowdrift, Billy and Rebecca were well on their way astride Bird Face, the troublemaker.

Rebecca laughed. "Whoowee! Was that ever fun. I ain't never had so much fun before I met you."

Billy didn't answer, but kept glancing back to see if the deputy was in sight. They veered off of the road and hid behind the First Mercantile Store. Crates and barrels stamped "Flour" and "Pickling Brine" were stacked high. A horse galloped past. They held their breath and watched the deputy tear down the road hot on the trail of no one.

Rebecca extended her hand, and Billy slowly grasped it. She shook it hard. "Nice work!"

"Same to you. Again, you help me. *Há-ho*, thank you, Orange Head."

Rebecca giggled. "All right. I guess if your pa can call me that, I'll let you, too."

A lantern flickered on inside the darkened store. The two crouched low. "Store's opening," Rebecca said. "Let's go before someone comes out here."

Boulder was awakening. One store window after another brightened as lamps were lit. Merchants in aprons shoveled snow from the boardwalks. The few children who lived in Boulder made their way to school carrying books and whistling, kicking tin cans in and out of snowdrifts.

Billy urged the horse into a gallop.

"I think I know where you're heading," said Rebecca. "Not sure I want to come along. And I'll be late for school."

"Please come," Billy said. "To me it is im—what is the word?"

"Important?" She closed her eyes tight, the freckles pinched together in a grimace. Finally, she nodded.

They rode in silence until they reached the tree. The cottonwood's branches looked more forlorn, sagging from the heavy snowfall. Snow covered the creek so completely that it was impossible to tell that a creek lay beneath. "What if they track us down here?" Rebecca asked, jumping from Bird Face.

"I must see father. This is only way."

No sooner had he said this than a chill wind blew from the north. Snow flew from branches, dusting their faces. Billy raised his hands skyward and tilted his face toward the tree. "Ghost of my father. I ask your guidance." He stood alongside Rebecca. Their unbraided, wavy hair—his brown, hers a golden orange—lifted into the air and mingled there like fire and earth. Rebecca trembled.

In the web of tree branches, a man's shape appeared, first hazy, then sharper. Bird Face snorted and pranced, but this time he stayed put. As the shape grew into the features of William Tull, Rebecca's gasp changed into a scream. She turned to run, but Billy held her hand and said, "Do not fear him."

Again, the ghost jabbed a finger to the north while his other hand grasped his throat where the noose dangled. Rebecca's body suddenly relaxed, as if she understood something. She stopped shaking.

"He's pointing in the direction of my house, where he used to live."

"We go there, Father?"

The ghost nodded. It flew to the ground, dug in the snow, pointed again, and then dug. "Something buried at house?" Billy asked. "You wish me to find?"

The ghost nodded, pointing in the direction of the Conner ranch.

"We find this thing, Father. We go now."

As it knelt in the snow, the ghost of William Tull seemed to relax, as if at peace. The noose faded away. The ghost began to fade into the tree.

This time Billy was not sad to see him go. "Good-bye, Father. I will bring honor to your name."

William Tull raised his barely visible hand in a farewell gesture. Then he was gone.

18 The Discovery

"What does your father want us to find?" yelled Rebecca as they raced toward the ranch.

"You not know?" Billy called back, feeling her grip tightened around his waist. He sensed her fear as they approached the ranch, knowing that facing her father probably scared her more than seeing a ghost. Horace Conner might even be dangerous if he caught the two of them together. He thought his daughter was in school and Billy Tull was safely locked in jail. Billy couldn't understand this father's anger toward his daughter. Cheyenne parents never raised a voice to a child, let alone a hand.

Fortunately, when the two arrived, Horace Conner was

on the far side of the corral, shoveling cow manure into a wheelbarrow.

"Let's start in your pa's old room first," Rebecca said. "My pa pretty much sold off all of his belongings, but it's worth a look."

Rebecca blew off a thick cloud of dust from atop the dresser. She glanced back at Billy with a sheepish grin. "Guess I haven't been in here with the dust rag since he died. I was kind of scared, after hearing of his ghost."

Billy opened each drawer. But all he found were mouse droppings. Rebecca peered under the bed and came up coughing. Nothing except cobwebs showed up on the windowsill behind the blue-checkered curtains. Billy crossed his arms and frowned. Then his eyes lit up. He wriggled his hand under the mattress. He felt around until his fingers touched a folded piece of paper. Billy pulled it out. It was a map with some words written above it.

Rebecca read out loud:

To whom it may concern—
If something should happen to my person, this map will guide you toward my few, precious possessions. Please see that they are returned to my

family who are camped on the Cache la Poudre River in northern Colorado Territory. They are my wife, Smiling Moon Tull and my son, Run Through Fire Tull. Signed, William Tull

They studied the map for a moment, then their heads jerked toward each other. "The barn!" they said in unison.

Horace Conner's head shot up as the two children sprinted across the pasture, Billy slipping and sliding in his ill-fitting boots. As her father charged toward them, Rebecca let out a whimper of fear.

Inside the barn, Billy turned to her as he pulled the shovel from its hook. "Orange Head, I fight your father. If I must." He jabbed the shovel into the earth, where the map showed his father's belongings were buried. A couple of furious digs later, he unearthed a brown cigar box, with an advertisement of a smiling gentleman smoking a cigar pasted on the top. He opened the box and quickly brushed aside the gold buffalo coins. He lifted out two pieces of tan, folded paper—just as Horace Conner came skidding around the corner. His tall, lanky form loomed in the doorway, face contorted in a purple fury.

"What is going on here?" he yelled. Not waiting for an

answer, he gripped Rebecca's bony arm so viciously, Billy thought he'd hear a snap. With his other hand, he slapped her face so hard she flew into the straw. Billy leveled Buffalo Bill's pistol at Horace, planting himself between daughter and father.

Horace's laugh exploded like gunfire. "You don't even know how to use that thing."

Billy ignored him and lowered his eyes to read his father's writing. When he gasped over what he read, Horace kicked the gun out of his hand. Both dove for it in the straw. Rebecca screamed. The gun remained just short of Horace's reach. Billy jabbed his thumb and baby finger into the man's neck and Adam's apple. Horace's eyes grew large with pain and surprise, then anger. He heaved Billy off of him and pinned him down with one strong hand on his chest. With his other hand, Horace grabbed the gun.

Billy grabbed a fistful of straw and crammed it into Horace's mouth. As Horace sputtered and gagged on the dusty straw, Billy kicked him. Curled in pain, Horace leveled the pistol at him, closed one eye, and—

"Don't do it, Conner," said a voice from outside the barn. The sheriff came into view with his gangly deputy right behind.

Horace Conner stiffened but didn't turn around. "This don't concern you, Sheriff," he said over his shoulder in a gruff voice.

"You kill that boy, and it sure as heck will concern me," said the sheriff.

"He's trouble, like his pa," said Horace. "Just like I remember you saying, Sheriff, before we hanged that injunlover, 'This won't cost the county nothing.' Same here. I take care of the boy now, there'll be no more trouble."

"You not pay my father. You kill him so no trouble," Billy said in an icy voice.

"Shut up!" Horace scowled, waving the pistol menacingly.

"What's he talking about?" asked the sheriff, now at Horace's side.

Until now, Rebecca had been cowering in the corner, tears filling her eyes. She had scooped up and read the two notes that Billy had dropped during the fight. Rebecca handed the notes to the sheriff and said in a shaky voice, "William Tull buried an IOU. Claims my pa owed him fifty dollars in back wages."

"Daughter, I'll take a belt to you," Horace threatened.

"She speaks truth," Billy said. "Read other note."

The sheriff wrapped his spectacles around his ears and read aloud:

This deed, on June 22, 1867, entitles the bearer, Mr. William Tull, to the transferred ownership of one Bay and one Palomino horse, this day, June 22, 1867, in exchange for past wages due. This exchange clears up any past wages due Mr. William Tull. Signed, Horace Conner

The sheriff's tone changed. "This your handwriting, Conner?"

"What if it is? Deed's worthless now."

The sheriff removed his spectacles and slowly folded them. "This deed changes everything. Appears William Tull was hanged for no good reason. You swore out a warrant for his arrest, knowing he owned those the horses."

"He was an injun spy!" Horace replied in a desperate voice. "He got what he deserved."

"That was never proven," said the sheriff.

"Believe it was *you* who started that rumor," added the deputy, removing the pistol from Horace's twitchy hand and slapping handcuffs on his wrists.

"You can't do this. You got no right! Should be him you're arresting," said Horace, nodding toward Billy.

"You had my father killed," Billy said through clenched teeth. "So you not pay him! He was innocent man."

Rebecca buried her tear-swollen face in her hands. "Pa, how could you?"

Her father scowled but said nothing as the deputy led him away. Rebecca sniffled and watched him until he was out of sight. The tears had stopped. "Your father's name is cleared, Billy," she said. "It's my pa who's the guilty one now."

"I have sorrow for this, Orange Head."

The sheriff looked amused at the nickname but said nothing. He turned to Rebecca. "Any kin, neighbors you can stay with while your pa's in jail?"

Her eyes were swollen and she chewed on a ragged fingernail. "The Watkins down the road have always been friendly. Mrs. Watkins came to help us after Ma and my baby brother died. But they got eight kids. And it's Christmas tomorrow."

"Exactly why Mrs. Watkins will be glad to take you in for a spell. You can feed the livestock on your way to school. I'm sure one of Mrs. Watkins' sons will be happy to help you with anything that needs doing around the ranch until your pa returns."

"If he returns," Rebecca said, her voice now sounding grown-up.

"I'll take you over to the Watkins'. Why don't you pack the things you'll be needing," said the sheriff.

"My pa's present—could I bring that by the jail tomorrow?" she asked.

The sheriff nodded. "Hurry, now."

"Billy, come with me inside," she said. "I have something for you."

19 Christmas Eve

"I know it's only Christmas Eve, but I want you to open this now, while I pack." Rebecca handed Billy something wrapped in green and red cloth, tied at the top with string. Attached to the string was a tag that said, "Merry Christmas to my best friend, Run Through Fire."

"I used your Cheyenne name, because that's how I think of you." She smiled. "That boy who rode on the snowstorm into my room. Into my life. And changed it … probably forever."

He cradled the wrapped gift in his calloused palm and said quietly, "*Há-ho*, Orange Head."

She smiled again. "Silly. You're supposed to say thank you *after* you open a gift. Open it!"

The cornhusk doll she had given him had blue eyes and two brown yarn braids hanging on either side of its cream-colored head. The legs were two narrow pieces of husks, the sides fringed like buckskin leggings. Billy knew it was a likeness of him.

"Your pa made the doll. It should be yours now. It will bring you good luck, I'm sure."

"Again I say, *Há-ho.* You are right, Orange Head. I am your friend. Always." He didn't dare touch her or even smile. Braves did not do such things. He decided to make her a gift tonight for her special holiday, Christmas.

As if reading his mind, she said, "Say, why don't you come to the Watkins' tomorrow morning? Christmas is a time for friends, so I ain't going to take no for an answer."

He nodded. "Then I leave. Still I must free my people. My father gone. I must find another way."

She frowned. "How? You're only one boy."

No, not a boy. He was a warrior, fulfilling what his spirit guide had told him during his vision quest. He had survived not one, but two massacres upon his people, the Cheyenne. He had cleared his father's name. His boyhood was left behind on the road like a shed snakeskin.

"You saw the poster that says they're looking for you.

The army doesn't give up easily. You're their *coup*. They'll darn sure find you. When they find out your pa's dead—and they will—you'll be sent somewhere else so they can boast they saved you from the injuns. And then—" Her words tumbled over each other like fighting cats. He had to interrupt and calm her before she popped a freckle.

"I see you when next the sun comes," he said with a nod.

20 Christmas Day

A robin's sweet trill filtered through the cabin's broken windowpane, heralding a brilliant, blue morning. Billy had been allowed to return to the miner's cabin and stay as long as he wanted. But he had slept beyond dawn, which made him angry. He knuckled the sleep from his eyes and climbed off the lumpy mattress. He should have slept on the dirt floor, but, without buffalo robes, he tried the white man's bed. His sore back caused him to regret his decision.

By now, he should have been to the house where Orange Head stayed, delivered a gift he had made for Rebecca, and been on his way. First stop would be Denver, to search for this friend of the Indians he'd heard Chief Black Kettle speak of, Major Wynkoop. This white man had helped the Indians. Maybe he could help Billy in freeing his people. It was his last hope.

As Billy rode into town, he saw women in bonnets sitting next to men in black hats and capes as they drove off in big-wheeled carriages and wagons, away from the bricked church. Some even smiled or nodded to Billy. Yes, this holiday of Christmas must be special for these white folk, who greeted him with a kindness not usually extended toward a half-Cheyenne. News of his father being wrongly hanged had traveled like the wind in the town. These people now seemed to accept him. In the white man's fashion, he tipped his hat to them, then turned north up the road to the Watkins' home.

The Watkins' ranch was just a short way from the Conners' place. Smoke curled from the stone chimney, and an evergreen wreath hung from the door. Candles glowed inside snow-caked windows. As Billy raised his hand to knock, children's laughter rose from inside. His stomach jiggled nervously, and he lowered his hand without knocking. Who was he to interrupt this special holiday of these people he knew nothing about? What had he brought but this flute he'd made for Orange Head? Would she laugh at his gift?

The door swung open. Orange Head beamed in her red pinafore dress, her flame-colored hair harnessed in a matching bow. Billy's stomach jiggled again but in a different way this time.

"I saw Bird Face tethered out there and wondered when you was going to knock. Did you think we'd somehow see you right through the door?" she teased.

Billy's face relaxed and he smiled. From behind his back, he presented a flute and nodded his head for her to take it. She blinked hard, color rising beneath the freckles. "You *made* this for me?"

"In our village, it is something a boy will make for a girl."

"*Há-ho?* Isn't that how you say 'thank you'?"

His eyes fixed on hers. He nodded and remained emotionless, careful to retain the look of a warrior, chin lifted, and mouth set. She invited him inside. When he hesitated, a small, frail-looking woman came to the door. Two children clutched her faded brown skirt. Each child sucked fiercely on a peppermint stick.

"Merry Christmas," said the woman. "You must be Billy Tull. Do come in. Rebecca's told us all about you. I'm Mrs. Watkins."

"I ... I not stay long," he stammered, as Mrs. Watkins nudged him in.

Her small head drew back in dismay. "Boy, we hurried from church so as not to miss you. After Rebecca told us the tale, we had to meet you. Least you can do is stay awhile."

Mrs. Watkins seemed to accept his silence as agreement. "We're sorry about your pa, boy. And poor Rebecca here, with her pa in jail." As she shook her head, the graying ringlets bobbed around her thin face. "But today is the birth of the Christ Child. A day only for happy thoughts. Isn't that right, children?"

One of the taller boys stepped forward. "Ma, aren't you going to ask him?"

"Oh, heavens! Well, I suppose so. Still say it sounds like nonsense. My boys here want you to tell us about the ghost."

Rebecca sensed how awkward Billy felt talking about his father in this way. Quickly, she said, "Oh, Billy, is that the cornhusk doll your pa made? Show it to everyone."

Billy forgot he still had the cornhusk doll peeking out from his coat pocket. He showed it to the family, and the littlest girl took it from him. "It looks like you. Is it you, Billy Tull?" she asked, wide-eyed.

He explained how his father had made the doll for Rebecca and how she, in turn, had given it to Billy for good luck.

"You'll need it around these parts, fella," said one of the older boys in a tough voice. "Folks aren't too appreciative of injuns—even half ones."

Mrs. Watkins softened the conversation. "Now, son, it's Christmas morning. Let's only speak kindly to each other. Pick up the banjo and play us a tune?"

The Watkins children clapped their hands and urged him to play. Rebecca turned to Billy. "He's been that way ever since Mr. Watkins died three years ago. Went back east in '65 to fight alongside his brothers in the Civil War. You'd think he'd be kinder to another boy who'd lost his pa."

"He has no reason for kindness," Billy said matter-of-factly.

The roasted chestnuts Rebecca offered him tasted like the nuts his mother had gathered with other Cheyenne women last summer. Summer seemed so long ago. The memory urged him to be on his way. Between bites, he said, "He is right. I will need the luck of my father's doll on journey."

A knock at the door made him jump. The banjo strumming and singing stopped. "Now who could that be?" wondered Mrs. Watkins, while lighting the last candle on the tree. "St. Nick has already come and gone." She opened the door.

The man filling the doorway brought gasps all around.

Billy's eyes frantically searched for somewhere to hide.

"It's Buffalo Bill!" squealed one of the children.

"Lord, almighty!" said Mrs. Watkins, her hand flying to the necklace at her throat. "Surely you're at the wrong house, Mr. Cody?"

"Don't believe so," he replied, "since that's the boy I'm looking for right there." He pointed the glove with dried blood at Billy. Gasps again, but Rebecca's could be heard over all of them.

"You can't take him!" she cried. "He's done nothing wrong."

"Didn't say he did," Buffalo Bill replied. He removed his hat and swept it across the front of his buckskin coat. "May I come in, ma'am?"

Mrs. Watkins hadn't taken her eyes off the man who was at least two heads taller than she. She blinked hard and stammered, "Oh, yes, of course. What am I thinking?"

When Buffalo Bill entered, Billy knew it was all over. He was a prisoner once again. He gathered himself up to face his foe, but something about Buffalo Bill's manner softened his worry.

"You got me in a heap of trouble, son, taking off like you did from Fort Lyon. General Custer was all for tracking you down. Then he figured you'd probably been killed along the way and it wasn't worth—."

"Did you really kill millions and millions of buffalo?" one small boy interrupted.

"A few less than that," Buffalo Bill replied, with a half smile.

"Why then you come after me?" Billy asked, wondering why the man still tracked him down despite the cancelled orders.

"I remembered how you saved my life from those Cheyenne Dog Soldiers, Billy. My hand's healing nicely, too, thanks to you. Even though you stole my gun, I've decided to forgive you."

"What is this word, *forgive*?" Billy asked.

"Means I'm not returning you to Fort Lyon."

Billy looked confused, so Buffalo Bill continued. "Last night, when I rode into town, the innkeeper told me how you'd found out the truth about your father's death. And the man to blame's arrested."

"My pa," Rebecca said, head lowered.

"I am sorry, missy," he said. "But I don't expect much will come of it. Right or wrong, I heard he'll probably be out of jail in a few days, and you and your pa can go home."

Rebecca rolled in her bottom lip as if stopping herself from saying she was afraid of her father. Billy had suspected that Horace Conner would be freed. The whites often went unpunished.

"Orange Head, I wish no pain to you. But he caused my father death. He should be punished. I have failed."

"No you haven't," Rebecca insisted. "Because of your bravery, William Tull can rest in peace. Because of you, everyone now knows he was innocent."

"I have something that ought to cheer you," Buffalo Bill said, waving a piece of paper in front of Billy's nose. "Would you like me to read it to you?" he asked, grinning.

"I can read a little. But you will do it," Billy said.

Buffalo Bill cleared his throat. "It's from the Office of Indian Affairs."

Proclamation to release the prisoners held in Fort Morgan, this day of December 20, 1868. All prisoners of the Washita River Battle are hereby released to the custody of William Cody, to be transported to the Black Cloud Reservation.

"It's signed by the Commissioner of Indian Affairs, Department of the Interior, Washington City. All true and legal," Cody finished.

"Washington City, where the Great White Father lives?" Billy asked.

"Yes, President Andrew Johnson lives there," said Cody. "Washington City is where all the big decisions are made."

"I made plan. Go to Denver to see white man who helps Indian. Major Wynkoop. Now, no need."

"In more ways than one," Buffalo Bill said wryly. "Major Wynkoop resigned soon after the Washita River Battle."

Billy smiled. "My people will be free then?"

"That's right."

"I will come with you," Billy said.

Buffalo Bill scratched his goatee and paused a moment. "I have something to ask you, Billy."

"You help free my people. I will do what you ask."

"I'm going to start up a traveling show soon. Been thinking on it. And I'm going to call it Buffalo Bill's Wild West Show. It's going to be big. Folks back east will pay to see buffalo, and bucking broncos and Indians and cowboys play-fighting. I've even talked a friend of mine, Annie Oakley, into joining up to show off her sharp-shooting talents.

"I could use someone with your skill with horses, Billy. What do you say?"

"What is *show*? Why with Indians?" Billy asked.

"A show is a little like your ceremonies, only folks pay money to see it. A show has music, dancing, and celebration. Folks want to see Indians—as long as it's all play-acting, not shooting arrows through their doors." The upward tilt of Buffalo Bill's moustache suggested a smile. "You'll be paid well enough to bring home money for your mother and goods for your people."

"I must see my people safe, on new reservation. Only then I join show. I have trust for you. Paper by white man, not so much trust."

"Paper by white man is better than white man's word. But I understand your mistrust," Buffalo Bill

143

admitted. "Let's be off, then. They pulled me from the winter campaign to get the Cheyenne moved onto a new reservation. Thought you'd want to go with me, though, so I took this side trip. Even though Custer believes you dead, I knew I'd find you here. He just didn't know the kind of boy he was dealing with. But I knew you were a survivor. And I knew you'd be the kind of kid I wanted for the show."

"If he finds I live?" Billy asked.

"You'll be working for me. Custer's got more important fish to fry than some runaway boy."

"Can't you stay here a little longer?" Rebecca begged Billy.

"I came here to help free my people. Now, I must go. They have long waited my return."

Tears swam in her eyes. "I'll miss you. Will I see you again?"

"Come to the show when it rolls through town," Buffalo Bill offered cheerfully. "Might be awhile, but we'll get to Boulder or Denver."

"I don't know where I'll be. If I'm with my pa, I doubt he'll let me come see you."

"Then I find you." Billy nodded his determination.

Rebecca beamed. She went to hug him, but dropped her arms when she noticed Billy's stiff posture.

The Watkins children trailed after Buffalo Bill as he walked outside with Billy and Rebecca into the brilliant sunshine.

Billy swung onto Bird Face's back. The pony nickered and tossed his head into the air, as if raring for a new adventure. Buffalo Bill climbed atop Brigham, tipped his hat to Mrs. Watkins, and thanked her for the beef sandwiches she'd made for the trail.

Mrs. Watkins blushed. "Why, sir, it's the least I can do for a gentleman as famous as you."

"Don't forget what you said, Billy! About coming back!" Rebecca chided, but then she smiled.

"Orange Head, sometimes you act more like brave than girl! But I *forgive* you." Everyone laughed.

"Good-bye, my friend," Billy said to her. He held up one hand. "*E-peva'e.* Thank you for helping me to find truth."

"It was mostly you," Rebecca said, "and you're welcome."

"Merry Christmas, folks," Buffalo Bill called as he spurred Brigham into a trot.

Billy preferred not to look back. Riding alongside Buffalo Bill, he fixed his gaze onto the great, white prairie that lay ahead.

Author's Note

As in all works of historical fiction, some facts and characters have been altered to fit the story. This note will let you, the reader, know what was real and what I made up.

The Washita River Massacre really happened on November 27, 1868, almost four years to the day after the Sand Creek Massacre on November 29, 1864. About 150 Cheyenne were killed at the Washita. Historians think that more than 200 Cheyenne were massacred at Sand Creek. General Custer led the Washita attack against the sleeping Cheyenne, despite Chief Black Kettle's attempts to negotiate peace.

I named Run Through Fire after reading a quote from Chief Black Kettle, who was a real person, when he met with Colorado Governor John Evans. "We have come with our eyes shut … like coming through the fire. All that we ask is that we may have peace with the whites."

The main character in *Ghost Over Boulder Creek*, Run Through Fire, or Billy Tull, is fictitious. I made him up. His father is based on a man named William Tull who really lived and worked in Boulder, Colorado. I learned about him from newspapers printed in 1867. I decided that he should have a son (authors can do that) and, thus, Run Through Fire came to 'life'.

General George Custer, Buffalo Bill Cody, and General Sheridan were all real people. So was the Indian maiden Monahseetah, who had agreed to marry General Custer.

Rebecca Conner and her father, Horace, are fictitious, as is the sheriff and his deputy. However, the ghost story that involved them really was reported in the local newspaper. The details of the story have changed several times over the years, as ghost stories tend to do.